Anonymous

Rays of Sunlight for Dark Days

Fourth Edition

Anonymous

Rays of Sunlight for Dark Days
Fourth Edition

ISBN/EAN: 9783337253660

Printed in Europe, USA, Canada, Australia, Japan

Cover: Foto ©Andreas Hilbeck / pixelio.de

More available books at **www.hansebooks.com**

RAYS OF SUNLIGIIT

FOR

Dark Days

WITH A PREFACE BY

CHARLES JOHN VAUGHAN D D

VICAR OF DONCASTER AND CHAPLAIN IN ORDINARY TO THE QUEEN

Take wing my soul and mount up higher
Since earth fulfils not thy desire

FOURTH EDITION

MACMILLAN AND CO
London & Cambridge
1864

𝔈𝔞𝔪𝔟𝔯𝔦𝔡𝔤𝔢 :

PRINTED BY C. J. CLAY, M.A.
AT THE UNIVERSITY PRESS.

PREFACE.

Books of Comfort for Mourners are very numerous. And so common is sorrow in the world, and so various the mould in which human hearts are cast, that there is a demand, less or greater, for every one of them.

There may be those to whom this little Volume will come home with more truth and power than some of those which have preceded it in the same endeavour.

The effort to console must guard against many things, if it would be effectual.

Sorrow is a great test of truth. Nothing which has the slightest tinge of unreality, whether in the form of exaggeration or of affectation, has a chance of acceptance with

b

persons in deep trouble. There must be, as a first condition, the recognition of the existence in the sufferer's case of that which is hard to bear; and there must be, as a second condition, the presentation of that which is perfectly supporting, because absolutely true, to meet it, if a man would minister with any effect to one on whom pain or loss, anxiety or desolation, has laid a heavy hand. Too often there is an attempt to ignore the sorrow; to treat it as if it were made too much of; almost to reprove it, as if it were fanciful or voluntary. It is difficult for health and sickness, ease and distress, a whole heart and a wounded heart, to meet and sympathize: grief is suspicious of gladness, and is slow to be persuaded that he who comes to the house of mourning from the dwelling of cheerfulness can bring with him a just appreciation of the calamity which he seeks to soothe. To be able to *weep with them that weep* is a necessary requisite in one who would be, in the Divine sense, *a son of consolation.*

It is the first object of sorrow, if we recognize in it any object at all, that it be felt. If there is a remedial purpose in it, or if there is even a chastising and a humbling purpose in it, this can only be answered by the entrance of the pain itself into the very soul's soul. This is what an inexperienced comforter will not let it do. He acts, with his spiritual comfort, just as he thinks it wrong and shocking for another to act with his worldly comfort. He counts it a great sin to drown sorrow by letting in the din of the world upon it: but does he not himself seek to overbear sorrow in an opposite manner, by haste and precipitation in administering the remedies of

the Gospel? Truths which will be valuable
and efficacious a month hence, may themselves be inoperative and inaudible to-day.
And the wise physician, like Him whose
hand is working with him from above, will
abide and watch his time. He will be
satisfied, in the first instance, that the soul
should lay itself low and let the wave pass
over it. Its foot must touch the bottom of
the deep waters, before it can safely rise
again to their surface. All that we can
desire to hear from the rent heart, in the
first hours of anguish, is the simple con-
fession, *It is the Lord.*

And here sometimes is the defect of books
which would comfort the mourner. They
precipitate consolation. They do not convey
the impression of the writer's having first
suffered. If he had, he would know more
of the first crush and of the first bewilder-

ment of sorrow. He would not only make allowance for the difficulty of accepting solace, but he would scarcely desire that solace to be too instantly accepted. The certainty that God is at work; the "whatsoever your sickness is, know you certainly that it is God's visitation;" would be almost enough for his first lesson. He would know that in that one point there is not only a groundwork of infallible truth, but also an element of unassailable consolation. If I am in God's hands, then, whatever the process, whatever the end, all must be well. But if I am expected, when all life is a blank, to see it instantly repeopled with objects of interest and of satisfaction; if I am expected, when life is felt to be insufferably long, to respond at once to the call which reminds me that it is but for a moment; if I am expected, when calamity

is so real, and so strong, and so grinding in
its pressure, to say all at once that it is
a dream and a phantom; if I am expected,
when I am enveloped in the thick darkness,
not only to say that I doubt not that God
is in the midst of it, but that I actually see
Him there and can rejoice in His light;
then I say that you are too quick for me—
you are building me up before I have been
taken down—you are seeking to confound
what God ever discriminates, the night of
sorrow and the morning of joy, the time of
my wealth and the time of my tribulation.

It is because I think that the little
Volume now offered to the Christian sufferer
is one of greater wisdom and of deeper experience, that I have readily consented to
the request that I would introduce it by
a few words of preface. For the book itself
I am not otherwise responsible. Neverthe-

less I hope that a blessing will rest upon it, and that some who are in trouble will recognize in it, now and hereafter, the voice of a friend, who speaks that which has first been known, and would comfort with a consolation first received.

C. J. VAUGHAN.

THE VICARAGE, DONCASTER,
October 31, 1860.

RAYS OF SUNLIGHT

FOR DARK DAYS.

FAINT not, Pilgrim! one brief day
   Hold on thy way;
Let not things that perish all
   Thy soul enthrall.
Short the present; to thy home
   Soon shalt thou come;
With thy Father thou shalt find
   All to thy mind.

      FROM THE GERMAN.

......From the calm shores of the land of everlasting life, have I watched thee, my beloved child, toiling through the waves of this troublesome world......and now, because the night draweth on apace, and the darkest hour is ever before the morning, I have come to thee upon the billows, that I may be near thee in thy time of peril ; and behold, I am with thee in the ship !......Fear not; they who follow Me shall never walk in darkness ; thy footsteps shall not slip ; mercy shall hold thee up when perils encompass thee about ; and though the sunshine of this world's joys be dim for thee, in My light shalt thou see light.

THE DIVINE MASTER.

Whatever your lot on earth, is it not better than you deserve? and amidst all your troubles, have not you much to be thankful for? There are sadder hearts than yours; go and comfort them, and that will comfort you. Are you ill and suffering? By your gentle patience be an example to those who are suffering too. It is the selfish manner in which we live, engrossed by our own troubles, which renders us unmindful of those of others: we hurry through the streets, intent on some business of our own, heeding not the many little acts of kindness we could do for one another, which would send us home with a light heart.

Trap to catch a Sunbeam.

Mourn, oh rejoicing heart!
The hours are flying,
Each one some treasure takes,
Each one some blossom breaks,
And leaves it dying;
The chill dark night draws near,
Thy sun will soon depart,
And leave thee sighing;
Then mourn, rejoicing heart,
The hours are flying!

Rejoice, oh grieving heart,
The hours fly past;
With each some sorrow dies,
With each some shadow flies,
Until at last
The red dawn in the east
Bids weary night depart
And pain is past.
Rejoice, then, grieving heart,
The hours fly past.

Miss Proctor.

The case of the Apostle is an undoubted instance of "the effectual fervent prayer of a righteous man" *not* "availing" for the object desired; in other words, it teaches us that the precept of our Lord, "Ask, and it shall be given you," must not be understood as promising a direct answer to every prayer, but as expressing the certainty, that He who knows our infirmities before we ask, and our ignorance in asking, will, in the end, supply our needs with all that we require, though not with all that we desire, or think that we require.

The Apostle prayed not for wealth, or honour, or wisdom, but simply that a great impediment to his usefulness might be removed; and even this was not granted. And, in like manner, a greater than the Apostle had "offered up prayer and supplications with strong crying and tears," earnestly and in an agony, and the sweat as it were great drops of blood falling down to the ground, saying, "Father, if it be possible, let this cup pass from me," and yet the cup was not removed, and the prayer was not granted. If the prayer of Paul, and the prayer of Christ, were refused, none need complain or be perplexed.

STANLEY'S 'CORINTHIANS.'

Let us bow our souls, and say, "Lord, what wouldst thou have me to do?"...Then light from the opened Heaven shall stream on our daily task, revealing the grains of gold where yesterday all seemed dust. A Hand shall sustain us and our daily burden, so that smiling at yesterday's fears, we shall say, This is easy—this is light; every "lion in the way," as we come upon it, shall be seen chained.

MARY, THE HANDMAID OF THE LORD.

......None are so full of cares, or so poor in gifts, that to them also, waiting patiently and trustfully on God for His daily commands, He will not give direct ministry for Him, increasing according to their strength and their desire. There is so much to be set right in the world, there are so many to be led, and helped, and comforted, that we must continually come in contact with such in our daily life. Let us only take care, that by the glance being turned inward, or lost in vacant reverie, we do not miss our turn of service, and pass by those to whom we might have been sent on an errand straight from God.

MARY, THE HANDMAID OF THE LORD.

......In every trial of every kind, for every
one of us, is it not the same? The answer
may come sooner or later, the well of joy
for which the heart yearns may be opened
early in the pilgrimage, or not till near the
mountain-top. But surely, unfailingly, we
are drawing near the answer to all our
prayers.

MARY, THE HANDMAID OF THE LORD.

The skirmish may be sharp, but it cannot
last long. The cloud, while it drops, is passing over thy head ; then comes fair weather,
and an eternal Sunshine of glory.

GURNALL'S CHRISTIAN ARMOUR.

Il arrive pour chaque homme, une époque
de solennelle visitation......Le moment des
grands coups arrive tôt ou tard. Vous ne
savez pas pourquoi ce front s'abaisse, ce
visage pâlit, ces cheveux blanchissent...quel
affront, quelle déception, quelle découverte
funeste a flétri cette vie naguère encore flo-
rissante ; comment cette vigueur s'est changée
en une sécheresse d'été...*Dieu n'oublie per-
sonne—Il visite tout le monde.*

MÉDITATIONS EVANGÉLIQUES, VINET.

I would have every one carefully consider
whether he has ever found God fail him in
his trial, when his own heart had not failed
him ; and whether he has not found strength
greater and greater given him according to
his day ; whether he has not gained clear
proof on trial that he *has* a divine power
lodged within him, and a certain conviction
that he has not made the extreme trial of it,

or reached its limits.   We know not what we
are, or might be...hence the great stress in
Scripture on growing in grace.

NEWMAN'S SERMONS.

...Her Summer may be to come, even on
earth ; and if it should be otherwise or-
dered, she is hardly one to grieve for the few
wintry hours of this life, when she can look
forward to the long Summer's day beyond it.
   ...I believe it is a great blessing we do not
know more clearly what Heaven is like ; for
if we did, we should sometimes be scarcely
able to endure our life here, even when it is
the most blest.

AMY HERBERT.

Whatever discipline Thy will ordain
For the brief course that must for me remain,
Whate'er the path these mortal feet may
    trace,
Breathe through my soul the blessing of
    Thy grace ;
Teach 'me with quick-eared spirit to rejoice
In admonitions of Thy softest voice!

WORDSWORTH.

Guide our bark among the waves ;
    Through the rocks our passage smoothe ;
Where the whirlpool frets and raves,
    Let thy Love its anger soothe ;
All our hope is placed in Thee ;
    Miserere Domine !

WORDSWORTH.

Ye mariners, that plough your onward way,
Or in the haven rest, or sheltering bay,
May silent thanks at least to God be given
With a full heart; "our thoughts are *heard*
    in Heaven!"

WORDSWORTH.

A king was once hunting alone in a wood, when he heard a very beautiful voice singing very sweetly; he went on, and saw it was a poor leper; "How can you sing," he said, "when you seem in so wretched a condition?" The leper replied: "It is because I am in this state that I sing, for, as my body decays, I know that the hour of my deliverance draws nigh, when I shall leave this miserable world, and go to my Lord and my God."

RACHEL GRAY.

Pilgrim, burdened with thy sin,
  Come the way to Zion's gate ;
There, till mercy speaks within,
  Knock and weep, and watch and wait.
Knock,—He knows the sinner's cry,
  Weep,—He loves the mourner's tears,
Watch,—for saving grace is nigh,
  Wait,—till heavenly grace appears.

CRABBE.

Soul, commit thy care to Me ;
'Tis My care, to care for thee :
Carest thou? then care not I ;
Therefore in Me hidden lie ;
Learn in Me thyself to sink,
On thyself forbear to think.

FROM THE GERMAN.

Do men hate thee, do they love?
   Take from thee, or to thee give?
Do they praise thee, or reprove?
   Still untroubled thou may'st live;
If, whatever thwarts thy will,
Thou with God abidest still.

FROM THE GERMAN.

Let cares like a wild deluge come,
   And storms of sorrow fall,
May I but safely reach my home,
   My God, my Heaven, my all!
There shall I bathe my weary soul
   In seas of heavenly rest;
And not a wave of trouble roll
   Across my peaceful breast.

HYMN.

Sans la Croix nous ne pouvons rien ; c'est par elle que nous arriverons au bonheur éternel ; près de la Croix, nous trouvons un asile assuré contre toutes nos mauvaises passions ; donnons lui nôtre cœur sans partage et nous obtiendrons un bonheur sans nuage.

N'oublions pas que si d'une main Dieu nous impose la Croix, de l'autre main il en soutient le poids.

Heureux celui qui n'a d'amour que pour la Croix.

Anon.

My lifted eye, without one tear,
The gathering storm shall see ;
My trembling heart shall own no fear
While it can trust in Thee.

Anon.

Depressed, and desolate of soul, as once
That Father was, and filled with anxious
    fear,
Now, by experience taught, he stands as-
    sured,
That God, who takes away, yet takes not
    half
Of what he seems to take ; or gives it back,
Not to our prayer, but *far beyond* our
    prayer.

                              WORDSWORTH.

TO A SKYLARK.

Alas! my journey, rugged and uneven,
Through prickly moors or dusty ways must
    wind;
But hearing thee, or others of thy kind,
As full of gladness, and as free of heaven,
I, with my fate contented, will plod on,
And hope for higher raptures, when life's
    day is done.

WORDSWORTH.

Guide, from Thy love's abundant source,
What yet remains of this day's course;
Help with Thy grace, through life's short
    day,
Our upward and our downward way;
And glorify for us the west,
When we shall sink to final rest.

WORDSWORTH.

c

O Thou, whose all-enlivening ray
Can turn my darkness into day,
Disperse, great God, my mental gloom,
And with Thyself my soul illume.
Though gathering sorrows swell my breast,
Speak but the word, and peace and rest
Shall set my troubled spirit free,
In sweet communion, Lord, with Thee.
What though in this heart-searching hour,
Thou dimm'st my intellectual power;
The gracious discipline I own,
And wisdom seek at Thy blest Throne.
Let love divine my bosom sway,
And then my darkness will be day;
No doubts, no fears shall heave my breast,
For God Himself will be my rest!

BISHOP JEBB.

Yet, Lord, in memory's fondest place,
　I shrine those seasons sad,
When looking up, I saw Thy face,
　In kind austereness clad.

I would not miss one sigh or tear,
　Heart-pang, or throbbing brow;
Sweet was the chastisement severe,
　And sweet its memory now!

Deny me wealth; far, far remove
　The love of power or name;
Hope thrives in straits, in weakness love,
　And faith in this world's shame.

Lyra Apostolica.

As we pass beneath the hills which have been shaken by earthquake and torn by convulsions, we find that periods of perfect repose succeed those of destruction. The pools of calm water lie clear beneath their fallen rocks, the water-lilies gleam, and the reeds whisper among their shadows; the village rises again over the forgotten graves, and its church-tower, white through the storm twilight, proclaims a renewed appeal to His protection in whose hand are "all the corners of the earth, and the strength of the hills is His also."...... It is just where "the mountain falling cometh to nought, and the rock is removed out of his place," that in process of years the fairest meadows bloom between the fragments, the clearest rivulets murmur from their crevices among the flowers; and the clustered cottages, each sheltered beneath some strength of mossy stone, now to be removed no more, and with their pastured flocks around them, safe from the eagle's swoop, and the wolf's ravine, have written upon their fronts, in simple words, the mountaineer's faith in the ancient promise: "Neither shalt thou be afraid of destruction when it cometh, for thou shalt be in league with the stones of the field, and the beasts of the field shall be at peace with thee."

RUSKIN'S MODERN PAINTERS.

Always say a kind word, if you can, if only that it may come in perhaps with singular opportuneness, entering some mournful man's darkened room, like a beautiful fire-fly, whose happy circumvolutions he cannot but watch, forgetting his many troubles.

FRIENDS IN COUNCIL.

You will excuse me, if I ask you to look
out for the sunlight the Lord sends into your
days.

HOPE CAMPBELL.

Crosses are ladders to Heaven.

PROVERB.

Lord, it belongs not to my care
  Whether I die, or live ;
To love and serve Thee is my share,
  And shall be while I live.
If life be long, 1 will be glad,
  That I may long obey,
If short—yet how can I be sad,
  To soar to endless day ?

Christ leads me through no darker rooms
　　Than He went through before;
He that unto Christ's kingdom comes,
　　Must enter by His door.
Come, Lord, when grace has made me meet
　　Thy blessed face to see;
For if Thy work on earth be sweet,
　　What will Thy glory be?

Then shall I end my sad complaints,
　　My weary, sinful days;
And join with the triumphal hosts
　　That sing Jehovah's praise.
My knowledge of that life is small,
　　The eye of faith is dim;
But 'tis enough that Christ knows all,
　　And I shall be with Him.

BAXTER.

The true answer...to the difficulty which perplexed Job, lies in the probationary and disciplinal character of this life, which makes suffering not necessarily evil, and prosperity not necessarily good. The very same events may be good to one man and evil to another, according to their character; as the pestilence which is the final judgment to cut off one in the midst of his iniquity, may be a merciful deliverance to another "from the miseries of this sinful world."

BARRY'S INTRODUCTION TO THE OLD TESTAMENT.

Though rising griefs distress my soul,
And tears on tears successive roll,
And silent memory weeps alone
O'er hours of peace and gladness flown ;
Ah why, by passing clouds opprest,
Should vexing thoughts distract my breast?
Turn, turn to Him in every pain,
Whom never suppliant sought in vain ;
Thy strength in joy's ecstatic day,
Thy hope when joy has passed away !

Anon.

I looked unto God in the season of anguish,
When earth and its trifles could charm me
  no more ;
When pain and affliction had caused me to
  languish,
And the dream of my youthful existence was
  o'er !
I looked unto Him who alone can deliver,
Whose arm of omnipotence never shall yield ;
And I prayed that His grace might support
  me for ever,
My rock and my refuge, my sun and my
  shield !

ANON.

Du pain, un morceau de pain, de l'eau, un peu d'eau, est á la rigueur tout ce qu'il faut pour vivre; et des êtres qui, comme nous, ont forfait à leurs devoirs envers le Dieu qui leur a donné l'existence, et de la main libérale duquel ils tiennent tout, non seulement n'ont pas le droit d'exiger davantage, mais doivent regarder comme une grâce et estimer comme une faveur la part la moins large, la portion la plus minime des dons du Créateur......Pour des créatures qui ont mérité la mort, et qui n'ont que par grâce échappé aux tourments de l'enfer, ne pas souffrir continuellement et sans interruption, ne pas èpuiser et absorber, durant leur vie, tous les genres de maux et toutes les espèces de douleurs, est un privilége manifeste.

De quel œil donc devons nous envisager, si nous sommes chrétiens,......les moments de bien-être qui nous sont accordés, tant de faveurs qui, quelque courtes, passageres, imparfaites qu'elles puissent être, seront toujours

gratuites, puisque nous sommes et demeu-
rerons toute notre vie incapables de rien
mériter ?

GRANDPIERRE.

...Isabel Hood, a flax-spinner in Elgin,
earning rather less than twopence a-day, lived
in the garret of a small house, with a thatched
roof and a clay floor ; a small grate, and one
pane in the thatch ; but from thence might be
heard such utterances as these over an open
Bible : "Glory, glory to Him for His blessed
Word, and for the light which He has given
me on it. The valley of the shadow of Death
is called dark, but He is brightening up my
ways;—O what glory !"

SUNBEAMS IN THE COTTAGE.

I love the western sky, said one who was afflicted in spirit; it seems to carry my thoughts away to another country, and a brighter morrow.

There is often something so unearthly about the sky at sunset;—those golden rays, darting from behind the purple clouds, how full they seem of hope and promise!—and on stormy evenings, when the "sun sets weeping," and gives prospect of a dreary day to come, I love to think of those distant countries where every day he shines as yesterday in cloudless splendour; and the thought of those distant countries leads me onwards to "the Land which is very far off," where this earthly sun will have ceased to rise and set, and where the glory of the Lord will be the light in which we shall live and move and have our being.

ANON.

Oh, ask not thou, How shall I bear
 The burden of to-morrow?
Sufficient for to-day, its care,
 Its evil, and its sorrow;
God imparteth by the way
Strength sufficient for the day.

THE DOVE ON THE CROSS.

If thou wouldst win, keep still the goal in
 view;
Who looks this way and that, travels not
 true;
Mark well the rule; he that would reach
 his home,
Out of himself and all, with a whole heart
 must come.

FROM THE GERMAN.

Who his own will hath quite forgone,
  And done and borne the will of God,
What else he does, or has not done,
  His path on earth has nobly trod.

FROM THE GERMAN.

Where should our helplessness find strength,
  Our helplessness a stay,
Didst Thou not bring us strength, and help,
  And comfort day by day!

THE DOVE ON THE CROSS.

Who nothing does, and nothing wills,
  But only suffers, waits, and prays;
Temptations, trials, conflicts, ills,
  He quenches in the best of ways.

FROM THE GERMAN.

The way is long and dreary,
   The path is bleak and bare ;
Our feet are worn and weary,
   But we will not despair;
More heavy was Thy burden,
   More desolate Thy way :
Oh Lamb of God, who takest
   The sin of the world away,
                Have mercy on us.

Our hearts are faint with sorrow,
   Heavy and hard to bear ;
For we dread the bitter morrow,
   But we will not despair ;
Thou knowest all our anguish,
   And Thou wilt bid it cease :
Oh Lamb of God, who takest
   The sin of the world away,
                Give us Thy Peace.

                    Miss Proctor.

We are pilgrims to a dwelling-place of blessedness; and the light that streams through its open portals ought to suffice us as we approach them. An anticipated Beatitude, a sanctity that even now breathes of Paradise, a grace which is already tinged with the richer lines of glory,—these should mark the Christian disciple, and these, as he advances in years, should brighten and deepen upon and around him, until this distinction of earth and heaven is almost lost, and the spirit, in its placid and unearthly repose, is gone, as it were, before the body, and at rest already with its God. A being, already invested with a deathless life, already adopted into the immediate family of God, already enrolled in the brotherhood of angels, yea, of the Lord of angels; a being, who, amid the revolutions of earth and skies, feels and knows himself indestructible, capacitated to outlast the universe, a sharer in the im-

mortality of God—what is there that can be
said of such a one which falls not below the
awful glory of his position? Oh, misery, that
with such a calling, man should be the gro-
velling thing he is! That, summoned but to
pause for a while in the vestibule of the
eternal Temple, ere he be introduced into its
sanctuaries, he should forget, in the dreams
of his lethargy, the eternity that awaits him.
Oh, wretchedness beyond words, that, sur-
rounded by love, and invited to glory, he
should have no heart for happiness; but
should still cower in the dark, while light
ineffable solicits him to behold and to enjoy
it!

                              Rev. W. Archer Butler.

Pray, though the gift you ask for
  May never comfort your fears,
May never repay your pleading,
  Yet pray, and with hopeful tears;
An answer, not that you long for,
  But diviner, will come one day;
Your eyes are too dim to see it;
  Yet strive, and wait, and pray.

MISS PROCTOR.

This grey round world, so full of life,
Of hate and love, of calm and strife,
Still ship-like on for ages fares;
How grand it sweeps the eternal blue!
Glide on, fair vessel, till thy crew
Discern how great a lot is theirs.

STERLING.

OLD SELF.

I mourn for the delicious days,
When those calm sounds fell on my childish
    ear ;
A stranger yet to the wild ways
Of triumph and remorse, of hope and fear.

NEW SELF.

Mourn'st thou, poor soul, and wouldst thou
    yet
Call back the things which shall not, cannot
    be ?
Heaven must be won, not dreamt: thy task
    is set,
Peace was not made for earth, nor rest for
    thee !

Lyra Apostolica.

It is good for thy spirit, and greatly to thy advantage, to be much and variously exercised by the Lord...And oh! learn daily more and more to trust Him, and hope in Him, and not to be affrighted with any amazement......O consider,...by His casting into the furnace of affliction, the fire searcheth; the deep distressing affliction which rends and tears the very inwards, finds out both the seed and the chaff, purifying the pure gold, and consuming the dross; and then at length the quiet state is witnessed, and the quiet fruit of righteousness brought forth by the searching and consuming nature and operation of the fire......Look unto Him. Help, pity, salvation will arise in His due time; Oh, look not at thy pain or sorrow, how great soever; but look *from* them, look *off* them, look *beyond* them to the Deliverer! Whose power is over them, and

whose loving, wise, and tender spirit is able
to do thee good by them.

ISAAC PENNINGTON.

I want to have no will of my own; I want
to have all my wishes and inclinations lost
in the will of God, so that if I see His will
apparent in anything, I may with pleasure do,
or suffer that thing; yes, do, or suffer it, as if
it were the very thing I liked best, because it
is the will of God.

MEMORIALS OF TWO SISTERS.

And now, above the dews of night,
  The yellow star appears;
So faith springs in the heart of those
  Whose eyes are bathed in tears.

AMERICAN POET.

To see a Christian mind encountering some great affliction, and conquering it ; to see his valour in not sinking, at the hardest distresses of life, this is a sight which God delights to behold. It were no hard condition to have a trial now and then, with long ease and prosperity between ; but to be plied with one affliction at the heels of another; to have them come thronging in multitudes, and of different kinds, this is that which is often the portion of those who are the beloved of God.

...The other consideration which moderates this affliction, is its shortness of duration. Because we willingly forget eternity, therefore this moment seems much in our eyes ; but if we could look upon it aright, of how little concernment is it, what be our condition here ! The rich man in the Gospel talked of many years, but, "Thou fool, this night shall thy soul be required of thee."

LEIGHTON ON ST. PETER.

The leaves around me falling
　　Are preaching of decay;
The hollow winds are calling,
　　"Come, pilgrim, come away!"
The day, in night declining,
　　Says, I must too decline;
The year, its life resigning,
　　Its lot foreshadows mine.

The light my path surrounding,
　　The loves to which I cling,
The hopes within me bounding,
　　The joys that round me wing;
All melt, like stars of even,
　　Before the morning's ray,
Pass upward into Heaven,
　　And chide at my delay.

The friends gone there before me
   Are calling from on high,
And joyous angels o'er me
   Tempt sweetly to the sky ;
"Why wait," they say, and "wither,
   'Mid scenes of death and sin?
O rise to glory hither,
   And find true life begin."

I hear the invitation,
   And fain would rise and come,
A sinner, to salvation ;
   An exile, to his home ;
But while I here must linger,
   Thus, thus let all I see
Point on, with faithful finger,
   To Heaven, O Lord, and Thee !

                  H. L. LYTE.

Take thou thy Cross, my Son; nor mayst
    thou choose;
The Cross I give is best—do not refuse.

THE DIVINE MASTER.

Renounce thy will; seek nothing of thine
    own;
Follow thou Me; thou canst not walk alone.

THE DIVINE MASTER.

O may this dying life make haste
To die into true life at last;
No hope have I to live before,
But then to live, and die no more.

HICKES' DEVOTIONS.

What an interpreter of Scripture is affliction! How many stars in its heaven shine out brightly in the night of sorrow and pain, which were unperceived or overlooked in the garish day of our prosperity. What an enlarger of Scripture is any other outer or inner event, which stirs the depths of our hearts, which touches us near to the core and centre of our lives.

Trouble of spirit, condemnation of conscience, sudden danger, strong temptation,—when any of these overtake us, what veils do they take away, that we may see what hitherto we saw not; what new domains of God's word do they bring within our spiritual ken! How do promises, which once fell flat upon our ears, become precious now; psalms become our own...which before were aloof from us! How do we see things now with the eye, which before we knew only by the hearing of the ear; which before men had told us, but now we ourselves have found! So that on these accounts also, the Scripture is fitted to be our companion, and to do us good all the years of our life.

DEAN TRENCH.

She may not say her all is gone, nor that her heart is broken; but girding up the loins of her mind, she must trim her lamp once more for the dark journey. "What, could ye not watch with me one hour?" is a rebuke which has many applications. This hour—the darkest thou mayest be called to pass through below—the greatest opportunity to glorify me, wilt thou pass it in the sorrow of the world, or watch with me?

THE WAY HOME.

......You have been wretched; yet
The silver shower, whose reckless burden
    weighs
Too heavily upon the lily's head,
Oft leaves a saving moisture at its root.

WORDSWORTH.

Poor wanderer of the world's entangled
    wild!
There is an eye that marks thy lonely way,
A heart that loves thee as a cherished child,
A hand that waits to wipe thy tears away!

ANON.

...You say that your sun has gone down while it is yet day; and that your path looks bleak and dreary in the gathering twilight. I know it, my Friend; I know that the brightness has vanished from your life, and that from henceforth you must endure hardness even unto the end.

But take courage; advance in perfect faith. Mercies you do not dream of now, will be strewn around your footsteps. Powers which till now have lain as sleeping shadows within you, will awake to life; powers of faith, of hope, of love; and of that perfect patience which will enable you to lift your streaming eyes to Heaven, and say: "Lord, I am Thine; do with me what Thou wilt; strip me of all earthly coverings; only save my soul alive." Then let the shades of evening fall; let your path be dark and desolate; but in the surrounding stillness, you will hear voices from the everlasting Hills, and the sound as of the waving of Angels' wings around you. One also, mightier than the Angels, will make His Presence felt, and as you place your trembling hand in His, and cry, "Lord, guide me, for I cannot see," there will descend a stream of light upon your darkening path, and peace so perfect, that with songs of Praise and of Thanksgiving you will pursue your way, willing to wait, willing to endure, willing to do all things, and to suffer all things, for His dear sake, who is leading you through the valley of the Shadow of Death, to the fountains of living waters, to the Land of everlasting joy.

ANON.

A little while, through grief and care,
Thy servants, Lord, their cross must bear;
Still let this thought our hearts beguile,
—It is but for a *little while.*

ANON.

He led me through the wilderness,
    A long and lonely way;
He soothed me with His tenderness,
    And fed me day by day.

Oh, better far the wilderness
    And desert way to me;
If wandering in its loneliness
    I should be nearer Thee.

THE DOVE ON THE CROSS.

Why do we seek felicity
  Where 'tis not to be found,
And not, dear Lord, look up to Thee,
  Where all delights abound?

Why do we seek for treasure here,
  On this false, barren sand;
Where nought but empty shells appear,
  And marks of shipwreck stand?

O World, how little do thy joys
  Concern a soul that knows
Itself not made for such low toys
  As thy poor hand bestows!

World, take away thy tinsel wares,
  That dazzle here our eyes;
Let us go up above the stars,
  Where all our treasure lies!

HICKES' DEVOTIONS.

It is a bitter consciousness when we are awakened from our youthful dream of happiness by some stern reality, and know that from henceforth it may never be indulged again; when an all-powerful, though all-merciful Hand has past over the beautiful vision we so fondly cherished, and its dazzling colours have faded beneath the touch, and we see that the form is the same, but the lustre can never be recalled. We may have thought that our minds are ready for the change; we may have pictured it to ourselves, and sorrowed for the inevitable hour, and even prayed for strength to bear it, but the experience of one real grief will teach us what no preparation can impart. It will shew us our own weakness, and the vastness of that mercy which stooped to share a nature endowed with such capacities for suffering. It will force us to look upon the unknown future with a chastened and a thoughtful eye; and whilst it bids us bear thankfully in our hearts the remembrance of our early joy, as the type granted us by God of the blessings reserved for us in Heaven, it will tell us that from henceforth the warfare of human life must be ours; and that till the grave has closed over our heads, we may hope but for few intervals of rest...

GERTRUDE.

Though smiles and tears, and sun and storm,
Still change life's ever-varying form;
The mind that looks on things aright,
Sees through the clouds the deep blue light.

ANON.

All earthly comforts vanish thus;
  So little hold of them have we,
That we from them, or they from us,
  May in a moment ravished be.
Yet we are neither just nor wise,
If present mercies we despise,
Or mind not how there may be made
A thankful use of what we had.

WITHERS.

The setting of a great hope is like the
setting of the sun; the brightness of our
life is gone; shadows of evening fall around
us, and the world seems but a dim reflec-
tion, itself a broader shadow; we look
forward into the coming lonely night; the
soul withdraws into itself; the stars arise,
and the light is holy.

HYPERION.

What though our bark a dreary course
   pursue,
We have the haven of our rest in view;
How grateful soon the calm which ne'er
   shall cease;
How bright the visions of Eternal Peace!

EAST.

Lord, as Thou wilt! nor this, nor that I
   will;
Lord, as Thou wilt, so only let it be!
Lord, I am Thine; Thy pleasure, Lord,
   fulfil;
I, as a child, will lift mine eyes to Thee.

FROM THE GERMAN.

In Christ's eternal kingdom, the distinction will be, who is the most like Him, who has done His work most faithfully......It is a comfort to reflect that our Heavenly Father knows all the circumstances of our trial, and appreciates every effort and every desire for sanctification and improvement......

......We have nothing to do with His arrangements; He sets us our work; we have to do it; step by step, day by day, be it little, or much, it matters not, so that we are but faithful; it will all fit, in some wonderful way, into His great plan.

BRAMPTON RECTORY.

"A little while," 'twill soon be past;
　Why should we shun the shame and
　　cross?
O let us in His footsteps haste,
　Counting for Him all else but loss.
Oh, how will recompense His smile
The sufferings of this "little while."

ANON.

Yes, I had loved this world too well,
　Each thought, each hope on earth bestowed,
Had I been left in joy to dwell,
　And tears of grief had never flowed.

Then shall I not with patience bear
　The trials that my God may send?
He will not leave me in despair,
　But bid at length my sorrows end!

ANON.

The believer may meet with storms and
trials, even where His Saviour commands him
to go; the path of duty is not always strewn
with flowers; it often passes through a bleak
and barren wilderness, in which the Rose of
Sharon cannot blossom, and where the Lily of
the Valley cannot grow. How frequently does
the Christian find himself on a rough and
thorny road, encompassed with difficulties
which no human skill can resist, and beset
with dangers which no finite power can over-
come; yet even then it should be enough to
sustain his fainting spirit, to know that he
is walking in the path which Jesus has pre-
scribed; in which He himself has gone
before, and which has been consecrated by
the blood, and marked by the footsteps, of
the Man of Sorrows.

"THE DISCIPLES IN THE STORM."

......Methinks if you would know
How visitations of calamity
Affect the pious soul, 'tis shewn you here.
Look yonder at that cloud, which through
    the sky,
Sailing along, doth cross in her career
The rolling moon. I watched it as it came,
And deemed the deep opaque would blot
    her beams,
But melting like a wreath of snow it hangs
In folds of wavy silver round, and clothes
The orb with richer beauties than her own;
Then passing, leaves her in her light serene.

SOUTHEY.

Although the day be never so long,
At last it ringeth to even song.

OLD SONG.

The Cross our Master bore for us, for Him
  we fain would bear,
But mortal strength to weakness turns, and
  courage to despair;
Then mercy to our failings, Lord, our sinking
  faith renew,
And when Thy sorrows visit us, oh send
  Thy patience too!

Bishop Heber.

It needs our hearts be weaned from earth,
  It needs that we be driven
By loss of every earthly stay
  To seek our joys in Heaven.

Yes, we must follow in the path
  Our Lord and Saviour run,
We must not find a resting-place
  Where He we love had none.

C. Fry.

I know thy sorrow—see thy daily grief;
I count thy sufferings, and do send relief.

THE DIVINE MASTER.

In every trouble look unto the end,
And take the Cross to be thy constant friend.

THE DIVINE MASTER.

Who loves the Cross, and Him who on it
  died,
In every cloud sees Jesus by his side.

THE DIVINE MASTER.

......For thirty-six years the victim of incurable maladies, often undergoing excruciating agony, sometimes for a long period blind, few have experienced the exquisite enjoyment of which her shattered tenement was the habitual abode; as she said to a friend: "My nights are very pleasant in general; I feel like David, when he said, 'I wait for the Lord; my soul doth wait, and in His word do I hope:' and while I am enabled to contemplate the wonders of redeeming grace and love, the hours pass swiftly on, and the morn appears even before I am aware; I experience so much of the Saviour's love in supporting me under pain, that I cannot fear its increase......I think that one end to be answered in my long affliction is, encouragement for others to trust in Him.

THE LAMP AND THE LANTERN.

My daughter—do not imagine that the work of your sanctification will be an easy one. Cherry-trees bear fruit soon after they are planted, but that fruit is small and perishable; while the palm, the prince of trees, requires a hundred years before it is mature enough to bring forth dates. A lukewarm degree of piety may be acquired in a year; but the perfection to which we aspire, oh my dear daughter, must be the growth of long and weary years.

JACQUELINE PASCAL.

The certainty that God will work all for good,—the seeing the dawn of morning from the hour of midnight,—the being able to detect the folds of the wing under the black shell of the chrysalis,—the seeing no single probable doorway to escape the difficulty, and yet to make no effort, but to feel sure that God will extricate; to see Isaac bound on the altar, and yet to believe that from him will spring a multitude...are signs of a living faith which few possess, while the reward is boundless perfect peace.

MONRO.

......It dwelt on her mind that for some deficiency in her Christian character this chastisement had been appointed. The language of her contrite prayer was, "Lord, what wilt Thou have me to do?" And He told her; and she became a mother in Israel: a sleepless, untiring benevolence was the striking lineament of her life. After the stroke of widowhood fell upon her, and she stood entirely alone, it seemed as if every vestige of selfishness was extinct, and that her whole existence was devoted to the good of others.

THE WAY HOME.

It is a dark and cloudy day for you! A storm has burst upon you; but you remember how, after the storm, the bow is set in the cloud for all who will look above to the Hand that smites them; the storm has come, and now we must look up and wait and watch, in prayer and faith, for the rainbow of promise and comfort.

MINISTERING CHILDREN.

......It was when the doors were shut, that He, who came to succour and to save, stood in the midst of His disciples......

DESTINY.

Oh thou, who mournest on thy way,
With longings for the close of day;
He walks with thee, that Saviour kind,
And gently whispers : "Be resigned;
"Bear up—bear on—the end shall tell
" Thy Lord doth order all things well."

ANON.

The day Thou gavest, Lord, is ended,
Recorded every word and deed;
May He, who to Thy Throne ascended,
Now for our pardon intercede!
The day is past, with joy or sorrow
Charging life's uncertain length :
May thy Spirit for the morrow,
Teach us hope, and give us strength !

ANON.

F

When these last hours of earthly bliss
    And earthly woe are o'er ;
These hands shall clasp, these eyes shall
       look,
    These lips shall move, no more.

Then let no tear thine eyelids dim
    O'er this pale house of clay ;
But think I rest at peace with Him,
    Who wipes all tears away.

These hollow eyes but seem to sleep,
    For oh ! to them is given
An endless watch of bliss to keep,
    For they have waked in heaven!

ANON.

"Now for a swifter race," was the resolve of one, over whose path sorrow was beginning to darken heavily : "Now for a busier and more active life," was the utterance of another, as he rose from his knees, after pouring out the bitterness of his grief into the ear of God.

THE MORNING OF JOY.

Is the cross heavy? doth thy sorrow tire?
    Never fear ;
When the refiner's gold is in the fire,
    He is near ;
Whom the Lord chasteneth most, He loveth best,
    Harming never ;
By Golgotha the way to heavenly rest
    Passeth ever!

FROM THE GERMAN.

F 2

All is but change below;
　　Nought sure beneath the sky;
Suns rise and set, tides ebb and flow;
　　And man but lives to die.

The sun which smiles to-day
　　Will fail to-morrow's sky;
The stars but gleam to fade away,
　　The world but lives to die.

Perish each earthly thing,
　　While, Lord, 'tis mine to stand
On Thine eternal Word, and cling
　　To Thine Almighty Hand.

Bitter I little heed,
　　All, all is sweet to me,
While I my hope can clearly read,
　　To live in Heaven with Thee.

Hymn.

To most men every year would render a pilgrimage of this kind more painful than the last; but Wesley seems never to have looked back with melancholy upon the days that were gone; earthly regrets of this kind could find no room in one who was continually pressing onwards to the goal.

* * * * * *

...On another occasion Law said to him, "Sir, you are troubled because you do not understand how God is dealing with you. Perhaps if you did, it would not so well answer His design. He is teaching you to *trust* Him, further than you can *see* Him."

* * * * * *

...She said with a lovely smile: "Oh, how can I fret at any thing which is the will of God? Let Him take all beside; He has given me Himself. I love, I praise Him every moment."

SOUTHEY'S LIFE OF WESLEY.

Where water takes its first leap from the top, it is cool, and collected, and uninteresting, and mathematical; but it is when it finds that it has got into a scrape, and has farther to go than it thought for, that its character comes out; it is then that it begins to writhe and twist, and sweep out zone after zone in wilder stretchings as it falls, and to send down the rocket-like, lance-pointed, whizzing shafts at its sides, sounding for the bottom.

Ruskin's Modern Painters.

Know well, my soul, God's hand controls
Whate'er thou fearest;
Round Him in calmest music rolls
Whate'er thou hearest:
And that cloud itself, which now before thee
Lies dark in view,
Shall with beams of light from the inner
      glory
Be stricken through.

ANON.

So spirits subject to God's will
Take all He sends with grateful praise;
And, bright or dark, they see it still
In love's own silver haze.

ANON.

STEPPING WESTWARD.

"What, you are stepping Westward?" "Yea."
'Twould be a wildish destiny,
If we, who thus together roam,
In a strange land, and far from home,
Were in this place the guests of chance;
Yet who would stop, or fear to advance,
Though home or shelter he had none,
With such a sky to lead him on?
The dewy ground was dark and cold;
Behind, all gloomy to behold;
And stepping westward seemed to be
A kind of heavenly destiny.
I liked the greeting; 'twas a sound
Of something without place or bound;
And seemed to give me spiritual right
To travel through that region bright.

The voice was soft, and she who spake
Was walking by her native lake;
The salutation had to me
The very sound of courtesy;
Its power was felt; and while my eye
Was fixed upon the glowing sky,
The echo of the voice enwrought
A human sweetness with the thought
Of travelling through the world that lay
Before me in my endless way.

WORDSWORTH.

Each cross hath its inscription.

PROVERB.

...Another fact that the dead would tell us is, that things which agitate the world scarcely reach the realms of the happy ; that many an event which the world sees not, or, if it sees, undervalues and despises, has its echoes in Heaven......

...When the soul of some poor beggar by the wayside, or of some poor orphan in the great Congregation, is touched by the grace and transformed by the Spirit of God, then there is joy in the presence of angels that such an event has happened. In Heaven, things are looked at only in the light of Heaven. Great events on earth are pressed into little bulk there; and what the world thinks insignificant occurrences, are there the grand facts and impressive phenomena...If God be not in minute and microscopic incidents, He is nowhere at all. If there be not a particular providence, there is no providence at all ; for

little things are the events and hinges on
which great destinies constantly turn.

DR. CUMMING.

Here, on the borders of that better Land,
Shall pain's sharp ministry for ever cease;
Then shall we bless Thee safely landed there,
And know above how good Thy teachings
    were;
Then feel Thy keenest strokes to us in love
    were given,
That hearts most crushed on earth shall
    most rejoice in Heaven.

ANON.

...But oh, it is not so; old age is a blessed time, when, looking back on the follies, sins, and mistakes of past life, too late indeed to remedy, but not too late to repent, we may "put off earthly garments, one by one, and dress ourselves for Heaven." Griefs that are heavy to the young are to the old calm and almost joyful, as tokens of the near and ever nearing time, when there shall be no more death, neither sorrow, nor crying, neither any more pain.

...Even though walking in darkness for a while, the aged have the sure promise, "At eventide it shall be light."

SUNBEAMS IN THE COTTAGE.

Be sure that you are in God's hands to deal with you as He pleases ; and then desire nothing, either in temporals or spirituals, but what He orders......

One great mistake of life is looking to the clouds for happiness, instead of looking above them.

ADAM'S PRIVATE THOUGHTS.

The generality of mankind create to themselves a thousand needless anxieties, by a vain search after a thing that never was nor ever will be found upon earth. Let us then sit down contented with our lot; and in the meantime be as happy as we can in a diligent preparation for what is to come.

ADAM'S PRIVATE THOUGHTS.

The oak strikes deeper as its boughs
By furious blasts are driven ;
So life's vicissitudes the more
Have fixed my heart in heaven.
All gracious Lord, whate'er my lot
In other times may be,
I'll welcome still the heaviest grief
That brings me near to Thee.

HYMN.

A wise man in abject want was eating some
garden stuff which he had picked up ; and he
said to himself, "Surely there is no one in
the world more poor and wretched than
I am ;" and he turned round, and beheld another wise man eating the leaves which he
had thrown away.

FRIENDS IN COUNCIL.

Look not mournfully into the past;
It comes not back again;
Wisely improve the present—it is thine;
Go forth to meet the shadowy future,
Without fear, and with a manly heart.

LONGFELLOW.

The disobedience of Lot's wife was not that
she went back to Sodom, but that she looked
back. Doubtless she verily thought that she
was pressing on to safety; but her heart was
not right in her. She was disobedient in will,
and in the hankerings and longings of the
mind......She looked back, and that forbidden
gaze betrayed a multitude of unchastened
thoughts, and a world of disobedience.

MANNING'S SERMONS.

She knew, for she had experienced, that for the afflictions of life there exists but one genuine fountain of consolation ; the assured belief that all our earthly sorrows, and our transitory sufferings are ordained by unerring wisdom, and infinite love ; and where this belief exists, the darts of anguish, however they may pierce, will never fix and rankle in the soul......We all set out in life with the hope of creating for ourselves a paradise on earth ; and all, sooner or later, live to mourn the vain, the unhallowed expectation.

DESTINY.

God has called you to suffer; and you go like Abraham, not knowing whither you go; like Israel, going down into the Red Sea, every step is strange to you. Still, be of good cheer, God marks your every step. He that loves you with an infinite unchanging love, is leading you by His Spirit and providence; *He knows* every stone, every thorn in your path. Jesus knows your way; Jesus is afflicted in all your afflictions, "Fear not, for I have redeemed thee."

One child of God was heard to say that if it were God's will that she should remain in trials for a thousand years, she could not but delight in His will. But this is not asked of us; we are only called to *suffer a while.*

M^cCHEYNE'S MEMOIRS.

G

Every stroke of the rod is but the muffled voice of love; every billow bears on its bosom, and every tempest on its wing, some new and rich blessing from the better land.

......This walk by faith takes in all the minute circumstances of every day's history; a walking *every step* by faith, a looking above trials, above necessities, above perplexities, above improbabilities, above impossibilities, above all second causes; and in the face of difficulties, and discouragements, going forward, leaning upon God., If the Lord were to roll the Red Sea before us, and marshal the Egyptians behind us, and thus hemming us in on every side, should yet bid us advance, it would be the duty and the privilege of faith instantly to obey, believing that, ere our feet touched the water, God, in our extremity, would divide the Sea, and take us dry-shod over it. This is the only holy and happy life of a believer ; if he for a moment leaves this path, and attempt to walk *by sight*, difficulties will throng around him, troubles will multiply, the smallest trials will become heavy crosses, temptations to depart from the simple and upright path will increase in number and power, the heart will sicken at disappointment, the spirit will be grieved, and God will be disappointed.

WINSLOW'S " PERSONAL DECLENSIONS."

Afflictions are in a Christian family angels unawares.

DR. CUMMING.

G 2

Perhaps the lot infinite wisdom has carved out to us, is in no ways pleasant to us; whilst others are walking amongst roses, enjoy all secular advantages, and are placed in the sunshine of prosperity, may be, we are forced to hang our harps upon the willows, and spend our few days in sorrow and grief. However, let us not even under these sad circumstances charge God foolishly, or be impatient under the severity of His correction, for this is no argument of the hatred of a Father. Let us rather in this case view the unspeakable reward, and the divine promises, which are sufficient arguments to revive our fainting and most languishing hopes, and able to form our souls to true patience.

THE BEAUTY OF HOLINESS.

There are thousands upon thousands, who, as far as the inevitable trials of life will permit, possess all the elements of happiness except the belief that they possess them. The sum of felicity would be multiplied to an extent beyond calculation, if men would make the most of what they have, instead of craving what they have not.

ANON.

Our hearts are fastened to the world
By strong and various ties;
But every sorrow cuts a string,
And urges us to rise.

ANON.

The great mistake of life is self-pleasing, or looking for a state of rest and satisfaction here, instead of taking up the Cross, labour in duty, and submission to the will of Heaven, with a renunciation of all worldly schemes of happiness, and patience for death to put us in possession of it. The only happiness of this world is preparing for it in another, and being content without it till death.

I never was happy till I knew that I could not be happy in this world, and consented to wait for it till God's time and place. This thought will keep me from all self-pleasing in forbidden ways; reconcile me to sufferings, crosses, injuries, mortifications, and put a smile on the face of death.

ADAM'S PRIVATE THOUGHTS.

God has only one way of bringing all to Himself; namely, by martyrdom, or the crucifixion of our wills.

God made us for eternity, and His aim in all He does is to bring us happily into it. Hence the necessity of pain, sickness, crosses, to break the strong chain which binds us to the world, and force us to take part with God in His grand design.

ADAM'S PRIVATE THOUGHTS.

Oh! shattered idols framed of fragile glass,
We thought were jewels! yet the day may
    come,
When every fragment which lies shattered
    now
May turn to sapphires in the land of
    Rest!

MONRO.

Better give my heart to God late than never; better by force, or the loss of earthly comforts, than not at all.

The "poor in spirit" are those who desire no earthly distinction, covet no earthly riches, are thankful for what they have, and think it more than they deserve.

It is hardly worth while to be happy for the short time of life.

ADAM'S PRIVATE THOUGHTS.

From strength to strength go on,
  Wrestle and fight and pray;
Tread all the powers of darkness down,
  And win the well-fought day.

HYMN.

There is a certain mellowness which affliction sheds upon the character; a softening that it effects of all the rougher and more repulsive asperities of our nature; a delicacy of temperament, into which it often melts and refines the most ungainly spirit. It is not the pride of aspiring talent that we carry to Heaven with us: it is not the lustre of a superiority which dazzles and commands, that we bear with us there. It is not the eminence of any public distinction, or the fame of lofty and successful enterprise; and should these give undue confidence to man, or throw an aspect of conscious and complacent energy over him, he wears not yet the complexion of paradise; and should God select him as his own, He will send some special affliction that may chasten him out of all which is uncongenial with the place of blessedness, and at length reduce

him to its unmingled love and its adoring
humility...The character is purified by the
simple process of passing through the fire.
"And when He has tried me, I shall come
forth as gold."

CHALMERS.

*   *   *   *   *

Thou didst it, who art gone on high,
    Where many mansions be,
There to prepare a glorious home,
    And deathless friends for me
Shall I rebel against the love
That fits me for my home above?
Ah no! e'en thro' this load of fears,
    My heart is springing up,
To thank Thee for the boundless grace
    That overflows my cup.

ANON.

There was once a slave called Æsop...
A Courtier, to whom the king had praised
Æsop for his obedience, answered: "Well
may he love thee, for thou loadest him with
all he can desire; but try him with some
painful thing, and then thou wilt see what
his love is worth." Now in the King's
garden there grew a nauseous lemon, the
stench of which was such that few could
bear to approach it. The King told Æsop
to go and cut one of the lemons, and eat
every bit of it. Æsop accordingly cut the
fruit, the largest he could find, and ate
it every bit. The wily Courtier said to
him: "How can you bear to swallow such
a nauseous fruit?" He answered: "My
dear Master has done nothing but load me
with benefits every day of my life, and
shall I not, for his sake, eat one bitter
fruit without complaint or asking the reason why?"

LIFE OF M. A. SCHIMMELPENNINCK.

So mounts the early warbling Lark,
  Still upwards to the skies;
So sits the Turtle in the dark,
  Amidst her plaintive cries.

And yet the Lark, and yet the Dove,
  Both sing, though different parts;
And so should we, howe'er we move
  With light or heavy hearts.

Or rather, we should each assay,
  And our cross notes unite;
Both grief and joy should sing and pray,
  Since both such hopes invite.

Hopes that all present sorrow heal,
  All present joy transcend,
Hopes to possess and taste and feel
  Delights that never end.

HICKES'S DEVOTIONS.

"If thou hadst been here, my brother had not died;" these little words plainly shew that these afflicted sisters both believed that, had they been permitted to order the course of events, the result would have been far happier. If something had happened which has not happened, the event might have been less wretched. O, how often do reflexions similar to this, barb the arrow of affliction with a poignancy which nothing else can give! These are the thoughts which in our wretchedness make us doubly wretched: "If we had taken such a course, if we had acted in some other manner, how different would have been the issue!" There can be nothing more unwise, perhaps few things more unholy, than reasoning thus. In dwelling upon secondary causes, we overlook the first great cause of all— the God of Heaven and Earth, who alone ordereth all things, and doeth all things

well. Has the Lord no share in the de-
cision? Did He not direct our present disappointment? Was He not present, when
our friend was taken from us? Duties are
ours, events are God's.

BLUNT'S HISTORY OF OUR LORD.

Did I not stand before my desolate hearth,
like one awakened from a dream, a vision,
exclaiming in despair..."Naked and forlorn
I stand amid the ruins of the past"? But
through the casement glided, in on me, as
I stood, the blessed rays of that eternal
moon—the moon that shone in Paradise—
the moon that promises a Paradise restored.

. PARABLES FROM NATURE.

You are tried alone ; alone you pass into the desert; alone you must bear and conquer in the agony ; alone you must be sifted by the world ; there are moments known only to a man's own self, when he sits by the poisoned springs of existence, "yearning for a morrow which shall free him from the strife."......Let life be a life of faith; do not go timorously about, enquiring what others think, what others believe, and what others say ...... God is near you. Throw yourself fearlessly upon Him. Trembling mortal, there is an unknown might within your soul, which will wake when you command it......

Every son of man who would attain the true end of his being must be baptized with fire.

ROBERTSON'S SERMONS.

Life is a long wish, and a longer disappointment; a bright delusion for a period, and a stern sorrow ever after. Blessed are they who look for the fulfilment of their expectations, not here, but hereafter: who fixing their stedfast gaze beyond the finish of earthly desires, the grave, look for the accomplishment of a higher and surer hope in that better land where sorrow entereth not, where sin hath no abiding place, where disappointment is unknown.

Zuriel's Grandchild.

I have mirth here thou wouldest not believe,
From deepest cares the highest joys I borrow.

Withers.

I'm watching for the morning star,
Oh, when will it arise,
To gladden with its radiance mild
These strained and weary eyes!
The night is dark, and gloomy, when
O when will it be past—
And the brightness of the morning
Glad the waking earth at last?

* * * * *

E'en now the time approaches,
E'en now the streaks of morn
Upon the dark horizon
With beams of promise dawn;
Oh night of sin and sorrow,
Of absence and of pain,
Thou wilt be soon the past, and never
Canst enshroud the world again.

Oh rapture too seraphic,
Oh bliss beyond compare,
When our Saviour and His chosen ones
Break through the glowing air;
When the groans of marred Creation
Are changed for songs of praise,
And Earth and Heaven in concert sweet
Their loud Hosannas raise!

ANON.

Hold fast to the present; every position,
every moment of life is of unspeakable
value, as the representation of a whole eternity.

ANON.

When obedience and faith are made perfect, it may be that knowledge and explanation shall be given.

And I do not mind now, Mother. When the sunshine goes, and the wet comes, and the river looks dark, and the sky black, I think about the Unknown Land......This is not our Rest! The river is rushing forwards, the clouds are hurrying onwards; the winds are sweeping past, because here is not their Rest. Ask the river, ask the clouds, ask the winds where they go to:—Another Land! Ask the great sun, as he descends away out of sight, where he goes to;—Another Land! And when the appointed time shall come, let us also arise and go hence.

PARABLES FROM NATURE.

...Lorsque nous ne regardons qu'à Dieu seul, nous nous déchargeons sur lui de tout nôtre fardeau, et il nous soutiendra......

Je voudrois suivre une carrière, mais il faudroit faire des dépenses auxquelles je ne puis pourvoir; je voudrois être prêtre, et la vue me manque; orateur, et je n'ai pas d'organe; chirurgien, et la main me tremble; voilà ma carrière manquée; ce dont je ne pourrai jamais me consoler: mais il ne sauroit y avoir de carrière manquée, si mes projets sont pris dans le plan de Dieu à mon égard.

Car alors cette impossibilité même où je me trouve de faire ce que je m'étois proposé, me prouve que ce n'est pas ce à quoi Dieu m'appelle; et les infirmités même qui m'arrêtent, sont autant de lumières par lesquelles Dieu me révèle mon cœur véritable.

MONOD.

It is of real importance to the circle around each, that they who are experiencing the undefined sadness of departing youth, should learn to sing as in the days of their youth; and that they, whose affections have been torn, or left lonely by the adverse circumstances of life, should be seen rejoicing because they have fixed them upon the home and the affections above.

"Work."

...But Patience was willing to wait.

Pilgrim's Progress.

"Are you not wearying for your heavenly rest?" said Whitefield one day to an old clergyman. "No, certainly not," he replied. "Why not?" "Why, my good friend," said the old minister, "if you were to send your servant into the fields to do a certain portion of work for you, and promised to give him rest and refreshment in the evening, what would you say, if you found him languid and discontented in the middle of the day, and murmuring, 'Would God it were evening!' Would you not bid him be up and doing, and finish his work, and then go home, and get the promised rest? Just so does God say to you."

......Let us take the full comfort of this *fact*, that we are servants, and have really no work of our own to do; nothing which we are striving to accomplish on our own account.

"WORK."

Her heart was full of bitterness; full even to overflowing. On a dark and stormy sea her lot seemed cast; she saw not the guiding star of faith over her head. She saw not before her the haven of blessed peace. The words "Thy will be done" fell from her lips; they were not in her heart... Through such moments of temptation and trial all have passed; and then it is, indeed, when we are not blinded by pride, that we feel our miserable weakness, a weakness for which there is but one remedy,......the strength of God.

That strength Rachel now invoked; from the depths of her sorrow she cried out to the Lord, not that her burden might grow less, but that her strength to bear it, to endure, and forgive, might increase even with it. And strength was granted unto her. It came, not at once, not like the living waters that flowed from the arid rock, when the prophet spoke, but slowly, like the heavenly manna that fell softly in the silence of the night, and was gathered ere the sun rose above the desert.

RACHEL GRAY.

Eternity! Eternity!
How long art thou, Eternity!
Who thinks on thee, to God will say,
Here strike, here wound, here judge, here
   slay.
Here let stern justice have her way—
Spare only in that endless day!

FROM THE GERMAN.

...And if, through His mercy, I too am permitted to look back from the precincts of Zion, through the long years of my past history, "on all the way the Lord my God has led me," it is not to mourn over the "burdens" or the "taskmasters," but to rejoice that they were made by God the means of my deliverance; so that, now at rest, and dwelling among "my own people," I seem well able to understand the glad response of those of old to the gracious injunction, "to shew kindness to the stranger," because they had been for a season themselves as strangers in the land of Egypt.

LIFE OF M. A. SCHIMMELPENNINCK.

The thoughtful heart that has survived many of its dearest hopes, cannot fail to notice a manifest intention of the Divine mind to destroy or abate every hope of man, except those which wait for eternal satisfaction.

...Let us not waste one hour in fruitless lamentation, for it is still day, and the time for successful work. That night, the hour of death, which surely cometh, when "no man can work," will make us sigh for a time as rich in possibilities as this.

THE AFTERNOON OF UNMARRIED LIFE.

Life is before you! from the fated road
Ye cannot turn; then take ye up the load;
Not yours to tread, or leave the unknown way,
Ye *must* go o'er it, meet ye what ye may;
What tho' the brightness wane, the pleasures
      fade,
The glory dim; Oh! not of these is made
The awful life that to your trust is given;
Children of God! Inheritors of Heaven!
Mourn not the perishing of each fair toy;
Ye were ordained *to do;* and not to enjoy;
Fail not for sorrow; falter not for sin;
But onwards, upwards, till the goal you win;
God guard you! and God guide you on your
      way,
Young warrior pilgrims, who set forth to-
      day!

MRS BUTLER.

SHINING STARS.

Shine, ye stars of Heaven,
On a world of pain!
See old Time destroying
All our hoarded gain;
All our sweetest flowers,
Every stately shrine,
All our hard-earned glory,
Every dream divine!

Shine, ye stars of Heaven,
On the rolling years!
See how Time consoling
Dries the saddest tears,
Bids the darkest storm-clouds
Pass in gentle rain,
While upspring in glory
Flowers and dreams again!

Miss Proctor.

A DOUBTING HEART.

Where are the swallows fled?
Frozen and dead,
Perchance upon some bleak and barren shore;
O doubting heart!
Far over purple seas,
They wait in sunny ease
The balmy southern breeze,
To bring them to their northern home once
more.

*　　*　　*　　*　　*　　*

O doubting heart!
The sky is overcast,
Yet stars shall rise at last,
Brighter for darkness past,
And angels' silver voices stir the air.

MISS PROCTOR.

Who would be God's, must trust, not see;
　Not murmur, fear, demand;
Must wholly by Him guided be,
　Lost in that loving hand:
Must turn where'er He leads, nor say,
Whither, O whither, points the way?

FROM THE GERMAN.

Fulness to such, a burden is,
　Who go on pilgrimage;
Here little, and hereafter bliss,
　Is best from age to age.

PILGRIM'S PROGRESS.

Weep not for broad lands lost;
Weep not for fair hopes crossed;
Weep not when limbs wax old;
Weep not when friends grow cold;
Weep not that Death must part
Thine and the best loved heart;
Yet weep—weep all thou can,
Weep, weep, because thou art
A sin-defiled man.

DEAN TRENCH.

When we pass through yonder river,
    When we reach the further shore;
There's an end of war for ever;
    We shall see our foes no more;
All our conflicts then shall cease,
Followed by eternal Peace.

HYMN.

......Weary deserts we may tread,
A dreary labyrinth may thread,
Through dark ways underground be led;
Yet, if we will one Guide obey,
The dreariest path, the darkest way
Shall issue out in heavenly day,
And we, on divers shores now cast,
Shall meet, our perilous voyage past,
Safe in our Father's House at last.

DEAN TRENCH.

He who God's will has borne and done,
    And his own restless longings stilled;
What else he does, or has foregone,
    His mission he hath well fulfilled.

FROM THE GERMAN.

Father, I know that all my life
  Is portioned out for me;
And the changes which are sure to come,
  I do not fear to see;
But I ask Thee for a present mind
  Intent on pleasing Thee.

I ask Thee for a thoughtful love,
  Through constant watching wise,
To meet the glad with cheerful smiles,
  And to wipe the tearful eyes;
And a heart at leisure from itself
  To soothe and sympathize.

Miss Waring.

I

...And of those three who sit there, one is a grey, childish old man in an armchair; another, a man who is not old, but whose hair has turned prematurely white with trouble and sorrow; the third, a meek, thoughtful woman, with a book on her knees, who sits silently brooding over the words her lips have uttered; for she has been reading how the Lord gives, and how the Lord takes away, and how we must yet bless the name of the Lord.

The good seed of those words has not been shed on a barren soil. As Richard Jones sits and dreams of his lost darling, he also dreams of their joyful meeting some day on the happier shore, and perhaps, now that time has passed over his loss, and that its first bitterness has faded away, perhaps he confesses with humble and chastened heart, that meet and just was the doom which snatched from him his earthly idol, and for a while, took away the too dear treasure of his heart.

And Rachel Gray, too, has her thoughts. As she looks at her father, and, whilst thankful for what she has obtained, as she yet longs perhaps for the full gift she never can possess...a sweet and secret voice replies: "You had set your heart on human love; and because you had set your heart upon it, it was not granted to you."

RACHEL GRAY.

Go, when the morning shineth,
  Go, when the noon is bright;
Go, when the eve declineth,
  Go, in the hush of night;
Go, with pure mind and feeling,
And in thy chamber kneeling,
  Do thou in secret pray.

Whene'er thou pin'st in sadness,
  Before His footstool fall;
Remember in thy gladness
  His grace who gave thee all.
Oh, not a joy or blessing
  With this can we compare,
The power that He has given us
  To lift our souls in prayer.

                              Hymn.

We must not think we need only to be *'supported'* under our affliction. Those who are pressing forwards to a better country, will not rest unless they are also *sanctified* by it; unless each successive wave that passes over them, sweeps from their souls some of the dross of earth, and leaves some gift of heaven in its room; so that the "changes and chances of this mortal life" shall be ever lifting them further from the earth, and nearer, ever nearer, to the Land of everlasting Peace.

ANON.

All my life I still have found,
   And I will forget it never,
Every sorrow hath its bound,
   And no cross endures for ever.
After all the winter's snows
   Comes sweet summer back again;
Patient souls ne'er wait in vain,
   Joy is given for all their woes.
All things else have but their day,
God's love only lasts for aye.

LYRA GERMANICA.

*   *   *   *   *   *

In awe she listened, and the shade
   Passed from her soul away;
In low and trembling voice she cried,
   "Lord, help me to obey!
Break Thou the chains of earth, O Lord,
   That bind and hold my heart;
Let it be Thine, and Thine alone,
   Let none with Thee have part.

"Send down, O Lord, Thy sacred fire!
   Consume and cleanse the sin
That lingers still within its depths;
   Let heavenly love begin.
That sacred flame Thy saints have known,
   Kindle, O Lord, in me;
Thou above all the rest for ever,
   And all the rest in Thee."

The blessing fell upon her soul;
  Her angel by her side
Knew that the hour of peace was come;
  Her soul was purified.
The shadows fell from roof and arch,
  Dim was the incensed air,
But peace went with her as she left
  The sacred Presence there!

MISS PROCTOR.

The darling of thine heart resign
  Into His hands with ready will;
Else shall thy soul with sickness pine,
  And anguish will torment thee still.

FROM THE GERMAN.

Cometh sunshine after rain,
After mourning joy again;
After heavy bitter grief,
Dawneth surely sweet relief!
   And my soul, who from her height
   Sank to realms of woe and night,
   Wingeth now to heaven her flight.

    *   *   *   *   *

Though to-day may not fulfil
All thy hopes, have patience still;
For perchance to-morrow's sun
Sees thy happier days begun.
   As God willeth march the hours,
   Bringing joy at last in showers,
   And whate'er we asked is ours.

Once a pain, that would not cease,
Gnaw'd my heart without release,
Sorrow bow'd me 'neath her yoke,
Then in sadness oft I spoke:
  "Now no hope is left for me,
  And no rest, until I be
  Swallowed up in death's dark sea."

But when I was worn with care,
Filled with dread well-nigh despair;
When with watching many a night
On me fell pale sickness' blight;
  When my courage failed me fast,
  Camest Thou, my God, at last,
  And my woes were quickly past.

Yea, Thou, God, didst make an end,
Thou such help and strength didst send,
That I nevermore can praise
As I ought, Thy matchless grace.
    When I sought with anxious fear,
    And could see no refuge here,
    Lo! I found Thy help was near.

Now as long as here I roam,
On this earth have house and home,
Shall this wondrous gleam from Thee
Shine through all my memory.
    To my God I yet will cling,
    All my life the praises sing
    That from thankful hearts outspring.

LYRA GERMANICA.

To feel that we are homeless exiles here,
To listen to the world's discordant tone,
As to a private discord of our own;
To know that we are fallen from a sphere
Of higher being, pure, serene, and clear,
Into the darkness of this dim estate,—
This thought may sometimes make us deso-
    late,
For this we may shed many a secret tear.
But to mistake our dungeon for a throne,
Our place of exile for our native land;
To hear no discords in the universe,
To find no matter over which to groan,
This (oh that men would rightly under-
    stand!)
This, seeming better, were indeed far worse.

                    DEAN TRENCH.

Oh wail not in the darksome forest,
Where thou must needs be left alone,
But, e'en when memory is sorest,
Seek out a path, and journey on.

Thou wilt have angels near above,
By whom invisible aid is given;
They journey still on tasks of love,
And never rest except in Heaven.

STERLING.

Though strange and winding seem the way
   While yet on earth I dwell,
In heaven my heart shall gladly say,
   Thou, God, dost all things well!

Take courage, then, my soul, nor steep
   Thy days and nights in tears,
Soon shalt thou cease to mourn and weep,
   Though dark are now thy fears.

He comes, He comes, the strong to save,
   He comes, nor tarries more;
His light is breaking o'er the wave,
   The clouds and storms are o'er.

LYRA GERMANICA.

Arise! put on strength, O Child of my Love! gird thyself anew to the battle; for behold the night is far spent, the day is at hand, and the struggle must deepen, ere the victory be achieved. Take unto thee, then, the whole armour of God, that thou mayest be able to withstand in the evil day, and having done *all*, to stand; for thou hast been faithful indeed over a few things, but patience hath not yet had her perfect work in thee, that thou mayest be perfect, and entire, wanting nothing.

THE DIVINE MASTER.

To thee, O dear, dear country,
    Mine eyes their vigils keep:
For very love beholding
    Thy happy name, they weep.

The mention of thy glory
    Is unction to the breast;
And medicine in sickness,
    And life, and love, and rest.

Oh one, oh only mansion!
    O Paradise of Joy!
Where tears are ever banished,
    And smiles have no alloy.

Thou hast no shore, fair ocean!
  Thou hast no time, bright day!
Dear fountain of refreshment
  To pilgrims far away!

There is the throne of David,
  And there from toil released,
The shout of them that triumph,
  And the song of them that feast.

And they, beneath their Leader,
  Who conquered in the fight,
For ever and for ever
  Are clad in robes of white!

BERNARD DE MORLAIX.

K

Thou art with me, O my Father,
In the changing scenes of life,
In loneliness of spirit,
And in weariness of strife.

My sufferings, my comfortings,
Alternate at Thy will;
I trust Thee, O my Father,
I trust Thee, and am still.

THE DOVE ON THE CROSS.

So when the days of joy are past,
    And life's enchantment o'er,
When we have bowed to sorrow's blast,
    And hope is bright no more;
There still are mercies full and free
    Mixed in the cup of woes,
And where the mourner cannot see,
    In faith he onward goes.

Then weep not o'er the hour of pain,
    As those who lose their all;
Gather the fragments that remain,
    They'll prove nor few nor small.
The thankful spirit finds relief
    In calm submissive love;
Toils on in hope, amidst his grief,
    And looks for joys above.

DUNCAN.

Be strong to *hope*, O heart!
Though day is bright,
The stars can only shine
In the dark night.
Be strong, O heart of mine,
Look towards the light!

Be strong to *bear*, O heart!
Nothing is vain;
Strive not, for life is care,
And God sends pain,
Heaven is above, and there
Rest will remain!

Miss Proctor.

Oh, but life is strong, and us
Bears with its currents onwards; us, who
    fain
Would linger where our treasures have gone
    down,
Though but to mark the ripple on the wave,
The small disturbing eddies that betray
The place of shipwreck. Life is strong, and
    still
Bears onward to new tasks and sorrows new,
Whether we will, or no.

DEAN TRENCH.

God! Thou art my rock of strength,
   And my home is in Thine arms,
Thou wilt send me help at length,
   And I feel no wild alarms.
Sin nor death can pierce the shield
   Thy defence has o'er me thrown;
Up to Thee myself I yield,
   And my sorrows are Thine own.

Thou my shelter from the blast,
   Thou my strong defence art ever;
Though my sorrows thicken fast,
   Yet I know Thou leav'st me never.
When my foe puts forth his might,
   And would tread me in the dust,
To this rock I take my flight,
   And I conquer him through trust.

When my trials tarry long,
    Unto Thee I look and wait,
Knowing none, though keen and strong,
    Can my faith in Thee abate.
And this faith I long have nurst,
    Comes alone, O God, from Thee;
Thou my heart didst open first,
    Thou didst set this hope in me.

Christians! cast on Him your load,
    To your tower of refuge fly;
Know He is the living God,
    Ever to His creatures nigh.
Seek His ever open door
    In your hours of utmost need;
All your hearts before Him pour,
    He will send you help with speed.

Yea, on Thee, my God, I rest,
    Letting life float calmly on,
For I know the last is best,
    When the crown of joy is won.
In thy might all things I bear,
    In thy love find bitters sweet,
And with all my grief and care
    Sit in patience at Thy feet.

LYRA GERMANICA.

Dreary and long our course may be,
But oh, our God! it leads to Thee;
Thou art the light by which we roam,
Thou art our everlasting home.

Earth and its pain we still may feel,
But Thou art ever near to heal;
Still, as our day, our strength shall be,
For all our cares are borne by Thee.

Thy mighty arm to smooth our way,
Thy light to turn our night to day:
Onward with firmer steps we roam,
On to our everlasting home.

ANON.

...He is taken away, and with him all my joys have departed; new cares rush on, new troubles beat against me, and on all sides I am environed by perplexities, *and alone.* These are all that remain to me, now thou art absent; and alone I groan under the burden. Nevertheless, it is fit I should live, though in sadness and bitterness. Yet, though I be in heaviness, I repine not. The Lord hath shewn Himself at once just and merciful: "He hath given, He hath taken away"—and while we deplore the loss of our brother, let us not forget that he was given to us......Thou hast but called for Thine own; Thou hast but taken that which belonged to Thee. And now my tears put an end to my words. I pray Thee teach me how to put an end to my tears.

St Bernard on the death of his Brother.

Brief life is here our portion,
Brief sorrow, short-lived care;
The life that knows no ending,
The tearless life *is there*.

O happy retribution—
Short toil, eternal rest!
For mortals and for sinners,
A mansion with the blest!

And peace, for war is needless;
And rest, for storm is past;
And goal from famished labour,
And anchorage at last.

BERNARD DE MORLAIX.

THE RAILROAD.

I took a flight, awhile ago,
Along the rails a stage or two,
And while the heavy wheels did spin
And rattle, with a deafening din,
In clouds of steam, the sweeping train
Shot swift along the hill-bound plain,
As shadows of birds, in flight, do pass
Below them on the sunny grass.
And as I sat, and looked abroad
On sloping land and winding road,
The ground outspread along our flight
Fled streaming backward out of sight;
The while the Sun, our heavenly guide,
Seemed riding with us side by side.

And so, while Time from stage to stage,
Doth bear us on from youth to age,
The earthly pleasures that we find
Are met, but to be left behind;

But God beholding from above
Our lowly road, with yearning love,
Keeps still beside us, stage by stage,
From birth to youth, from youth to age.

THE REV. WILLIAM BARNES.

In the first anguish of the soul when it refuses to be comforted, the mourner is tempted to despair of the good of affliction, and to say, Can it *ever* be otherwise than "very grievous"? But presently, like Sabbath chimes fall the words on the ear, "Nevertheless *afterward*." So, in the faith of this "afterward," the stricken heart strives to endure in Patience that chastening which for the present is only "grievous;" content to sow in tears, believing that after many days the "peaceable fruits of righteousness" will be yielded,—Love, and peace, and joy in the Holy Ghost.

MRS HENRY BROCK.

...If thou wilt in truth go out to meet thy Bridegroom, it is fitting that thou shouldest first tread some portion of the path that He has travelled. Now whereas the Bridegroom has suffered shame, hunger, cold, thirst, heat, and bitter pain, for three-and-thirty years, and at last a bitter death, for the Bride's sake, out of pure love; is it not just and right that the Bride should venture even her life for the Bridegroom's sake, out of love, and with all her heart? Verily, if thou hadst the right sort of love and true faithfulness unto thy Bridegroom, all thy fear would vanish......But in these days those be few and far between who do truly go out to meet the Bridegroom, such as there were many in the olden time. Therefore it behoveth each one to look at himself, and consider his ways with great earnestness. For the time is at hand—nay

it is already come—when it may be said
of most who are now living here, that "they
have eyes and see not, and ears that hear
not." Dear Children, let us all strive to
enter into this wedding-feast, most rich in
joy, and honour, and blessedness.

......But there is yet another myrrh......
the myrrh which God gives us in the cup
of trouble and sorrow, of whatever kind
it may be, outward or inward. Ah, if thou
couldst but receive this myrrh as from its
true source, and drink it with the same love
with which God puts it to thy lips, what
blessedness would it work in thee! Ah,
what a joy and peace and an excellent thing
were that! Yes, the very least and the
very greatest sorrows that God ever suffers
to befal thee, proceed from the depths of
His unspeakable love; and such great love
were better for thee than the highest and
best gifts besides that He has given thee
or ever could give thee, if thou couldst

but see it in this light; yea, however small a suffering light on thee, God, who counts the smallest hair that ever fell from thy head,—God has chosen, and purposed, and appointed that it should befal thee...... Now sometimes people have said to me, "Master, it is ill with me; I have much "suffering and tribulation;" and when I have answered, "It is all as it should be;" they have said, "No, Master, I have deserved it; I have cherished an evil thing in my heart." Then take blame to thyself; but, whether thy pain be deserved or not, believe that it comes from God, and thank Him, and bear it, and resign thyself to it.

Tauler's Sermons.

Our beloved have departed,
While we tarry broken hearted,
In the dreary, empty house;
They have ended life's brief story,
They have reached the home of glory,
Over death victorious!

Hush that sobbing, weep more lightly;
On we travel, daily, nightly,
To the rest that they have found:
Are we not upon the river,
Sailing fast to meet for ever,
On more holy, happy ground?

*　*　*　*　*

Every hour that passes o'er us,
Speaks of comfort yet before us,
Of our journey's rapid rate;
And like passing vesper bells,
The clock of time its chiming tells,
At Eternity's broad gate.

HYMNS FROM THE LAND OF LUTHER.

L

It seems to be God's way, and we may humbly and firmly believe a kind and good way, to give His creatures heavy burdens to bear: to make all, so to speak, carry weight in the race of life: and work and fight at a certain disadvantage. There is some little thing about every one which holds him back from being a far better, happier, and more successful man, than now he will ever be. There is something in our nature, something in our circumstances, which is as the additional pounds laid on a horse's back, preventing his doing his very best: greatly abating the visible results of his strength and speed.

GRAVER THOUGHTS OF A COUNTRY PARSON.

God has given you a weighty share of the trials of this life: He has stricken you as though wilfully, less like a child one chastises, than as a victim one immolates, and still you do not seem to see the bent He has given you for Himself. If He wishes to possess your whole soul, can we be surprised that He deprives it of everything capable of leading it astray? The Gospel tells us He is a kind God. Those caresses of which you dream, that sweet and lawful love which would overflow like a balm from your stricken heart, those ineffable delights of pure affection of which men are allowed to get a snatch: why should not your Lord be afraid that these things would prevent you from loving Him alone?...You would fain harbour another profane love, and God, who perhaps does not will it, strikes and wounds you.

He crucifies you in order to get you to love His crucified Son more, and realize that crucifixion in yourself.

MEMOIRS OF THE ABBÉ LACORDAIRE.

Christian life is no bank of roses,
   Where we idly sit and sing,
Till the gathering evening closes,
   Christian life is an earnest thing.

Full of vows, and full of labour,
   All our days fresh duties bring,
First to God, and then our neighbour,
   Christian life is an earnest thing.

Onward, ever onward pressing,
   Yet untired as Angel's wing,
Believing, doing, blest, and blessing,
   Christian life is an earnest thing.

On its wayside none may linger
  Undisturbed by sorrow's sting,
Or by judgments' warning finger,
  Christian life is an earnest thing.

Wake then, Christian, from thy slumber,
  Evening doth its shadows bring:
Few the hours thy day may number,
  Christian life is an earnest thing.

PARISH MUSINGS.

Autumn hath violets as well as spring,
And age its sweetness hath as well as youth.

MARY MAYNARD.

Good Christian, onward, onward haste,
Dwell not upon the gloomy past;
Let not the mist of useless tears,
Shed over early doubts and fears,
Shadow the heart, or dim the eye,
That should look beamingly on high.

Let it suffice thee to have given,
So many years away from Heaven,
And let the remnant of thy days,
Be all one life of prayer and praise,
Too little for that glorious God,
Who bought thee with His precious blood.

* * * * * * *

Then onward, Christian, onward haste,
Dwell not upon the gloomy past;
Let not the mist of useless tears,
Shed over early doubts and fears,
Shadow the heart, or dim the eye,
That should look beamingly on high!

PARISH MUSINGS.

Mere courage, even if it be heroic after the human standard, often evaporates under slow *dis*couragement. But perseverance *under* discouragement,—the steady struggling onwards through hours of weakness—the rising upwards still above all doubt and fear—the eye fixed on the coming light in the midst of darkness and perplexity—the hard work continued notwithstanding opposition, distrust, disappointment, failing health;—and all this made harder by the bitter consciousness of sin, and by inward temptations which no one can fully understand but the tempted man himself—this holy tenacity of purpose is what we need, in this life of cloud and conflict, as much as anything in the world; and of this holy tenacity the Apostle Paul is an eminent example.

DR HOWSON'S HULSEAN LECTURES.

Were it not that God supports me, and by
His omnipotent goodness often totally sus-
pends all sense of worldly things, I could not
sustain the weight many days, perhaps hours.
But even in this low ebb of fortune, I am not
without some kind interval....

...Upon the best observation I could ever
make, I am induced to believe that it is much
easier to be contented without riches, than
with them. It is so natural for a rich man to
make his gold his god: for whatever a person
loves most, that thing, be it what it will, he
will certainly make his god: it is so difficult
not to trust in it, not to depend on it for
support and happiness, that I do not know
one rich man in the world with whom I would
exchange conditions.

The Mother of the Wesleys.

The art of life is more like the wrestler's
art than the dancer's, in respect of this, that
it should stand ready and firm to meet onsets
which are sudden and unexpected.

MARCUS AURELIUS ANTONINUS.

CHRISTIAN SELF-DENIAL.

Many a time it has gained victories, silently
won, in struggling hearts, to which earthly
battle-fields are nothing....What incalculable,
what inexpressible things has it brought men
to do, to suffer, to resign! It does its work,
even yet, amid the trimness of modern society.
Ah, my brethren, sometimes the thin check,
the deep-lined brow, the languid step, are
indications of a heroism every whit as noble,
of a strife every whit as fearful, as ever were
hinted by the empty sleeve, the scarred face,
the cross of valour over the brave heart.

GRAVER THOUGHTS OF A COUNTRY PARSON.

Hast thou a care, whose pressure dread
Expels sweet slumber from thy bed?
To thy Redeemer take that care,
And change anxiety to prayer.

Hast thou a hope, from which thy heart
Would feel it almost death to part?
Entreat thy Lord that hope to crown,
Or give thee strength to lay it down.

Hast thou a friend, whose image dear
May prove an idol worshipp'd here?
Implore the Lord that nought may be
A shadow between Heaven and thee.

Whate'er the care that breaks thy rest,
Whate'er the wish that swells thy breast,
Spread before God that wish, that care,
And change anxiety to prayer.

HYMN.

The Lord will draw us and securely lead us to Himself, in a way contrary to all our natural will, until He have divested us thereof, and consumed it and made it thoroughly subject unto the Divine will. For this is His will—that we should cease to regard our own wishes or dislikes; that it should become a light matter to us whether He give or take away, whether we have abundance or suffer want; and let all things go, if only we may receive and apprehend God Himself; that whether things please us or displease us, we may leave all things to take their course, and cleave to Him alone......

...Children, the place from which Christ ascended up to heaven was the Mount of Olives. This mountain had three sorts of light. The first was from the sunrise, for the hill is high and slopes toward the east; and when the sun no longer shone on the mountain, its rays were reflected from the

golden roof of the temple; and thirdly, on
that hill grew the essential material of light,
the olive-tree. So likewise the soul, in which
God shall arise sweetly as without a cloud,
must be a lofty hill, raised above these earthly perishable things, and be illuminated by
three kinds of light; that is to say, there
must be a place whereon the rays of the
high and holy Trinity can shine and bring
forth God's high and noble work in the soul,
according to all His will, and so that the
brightness of the eternal God may flow
into that soul. This mountain lay between
Jerusalem and Bethany. Now know of a
truth that whosoever will truly follow after
Christ, must mount or climb this hill, toilsome
or weary as the task may be; for there is no
mountain on the face of the earth, however
beautiful and delightful, but what is difficult
and toilsome to ascend........Now we find
many who would gladly follow Him without
pain or toil and as long as the path was
easy, and would fain be upon this mountain

on the side looking towards Jerusalem, which
signifieth peace, that it should minister
peace, and they should be without contra-
diction......They will not set foot on the
other side that looks towards Bethany, which
name signifies the pain of obedience or of
suffering. Of which place the Prophet says
in the Psalms: "Who passing through the
vale of Baca make it a well." Know, dear
Children, he who will not pitch his tent
in this valley, remaineth unfruitful, and
nothing will ever come of him......A devout
heart shall ever have a sorrowful yearning
after her Beloved, who has ascended to such
distant and lofty heights, whither the eye
cannot follow or trace Him. Hence, the
more truly and deeply the ground of a
man's soul has been touched by God, the
more truly does he find this valley of tears
within him......This is the meaning of the
side of the mountain looking towards Bethany.

Tauler's Sermons.

They placed him in his former cell, and
      there
   Watched him departing; what few words
      he said
Were of calm peace and gladness, with one
      care
   Mingled,—one only dread,

Lest an eternity should not suffice
   To take the measure and the breadth and
      height
Of what there is reserved in Paradise,
   An ever new delight.

                                    DEAN TRENCH.

There are sometimes sad awakenings from sleep in this world. It is very sad to dream by night of vanished joys; to revisit old scenes, and dwell once more among the unforgotten forms of our loved and lost, to see in the dreamland the old familiar look, and hear the well-remembered tones of a voice long hushed and still, and then to wake, with the morning light, to the aching sense of our loneliness again. It were very sad for the poor criminal to wake from sweet dreams of other and happier days, days of innocence, and hope, and peace, when kind friends, and a happy home, and an honoured or unstained name were his,—to wake in his cell on the morning of his execution, to the horrible recollection that all is gone for ever, and that to-day he must die a felon's death. But inconceivably more awful than any awakening which earthly daybreak has ever brought, shall be the

awakening of the self-deluded soul when
it is roused in horror and surprise from the
dream of life—to meet Almighty God in
judgment!

SERMONS BY REV. J. CAIRD.

Some murmur, when their sky is clear,
   And wholly bright to view,
If one small speck of dark appear
   In their great heaven of blue.
And some with thankful love are filled,
   If but one streak of light,
One ray of God's good mercy gild
   The darkness of the night.

DEAN TRENCH.

Shades of coming woe surround us,
 Springing up on every side;
Spread Thy sheltering wings around us,
 That in peace we may abide.

Darker now they gather o'er us,
 Like the shadows of Thy rod,
Stretching down the path before us,
 And we tremble, mighty God.

Suffer not our feet to stumble,
 Suffer not our steps to slide,
Keep us lowly, keep us humble,
 And be Thou Thyself our Guide.
     THE DOVE ON THE CROSS.

You stand on the margin of eternal
things; the immense ocean of eternity is
stretched out before you; you must soon
embark upon it. Time, how short! Life,
what a vapour!......Oh, then, let the consideration that eternity is at hand calm your
mind, and remove all your anxieties about
this world. The only material question,
"Where shall I lean my head, and lodge
my soul, and find my home for ever?" is
to you satisfactorily answered—"The Lord
is the strength of your heart, and your
portion for ever."

E. BICKERSTETH.

Another source of relief in sorrow, *There is a work to be done.* The night cometh; the eventide is upon us; the shadows are long. Work!......Is there no disciple of Thine, blessed Master, not one, to whom I may give a cup of cold water for Thy sake? See the state of my poor heart; see the weeds, the blight, the barren condition of the garden of my soul; and I would water it with my tears; I would pray for rain and dew from heaven. "This is not enough," saith the Heavenly Husbandman; "go *work* in that vineyard, and keep thy heart with all diligence. Weeping may endure for a night, but joy cometh in the morning: flowers shall spring; fruits shall ripen; a sweet savour shall perfume the air." Whence all this? It is the presence of the Comforter. He hath taken a lily from us, more than one. Sorrow hath filled your heart; but let not your heart be troubled. He will come this way again soon. He will gather more lilies. You need not fear, if you can say this: "I am my Beloved's, and my Beloved is mine; He feedeth among the lilies."

SERMONS BY REV. J. HULLETT.

Amidst the roaring of the sea,
　My soul still hangs her hopes on Thee;
Thy constant love, Thy faithful care,
　Is all that saves me from despair.

Though tempest-tost, and half a wreck,
　My Saviour through the floods I seek;
Let neither winds nor stormy main
　Force back my shattered bark again.

OLNEY HYMNS.

......Casting all your care upon Him, for He careth for you......

What a calm, what a peace, in the midst of a storm, does this gracious habit of godly dependence give to a man! Suppose, to-morrow, that you were expecting something very important to take place; and a heavy burden of care is the natural consequence of so grave an expectation. You are calm and composed, your mind is at peace. You have done your best to meet the emergency, and as a Christian, as a man of God, you cast all your care on Him, knowing assuredly that He careth for you.

And there is really a to-morrow of importance to every one of us. We shall have to unloose the bands of mortality. We shall have to take off our outer garments, and bidding good night to all about our strange and narrow bed, we shall have to lie down for the last time on earth, and let death put

out our light. Oh! what a happy thing
it will be for faith, the handmaid of the
Lord, to sound in our ear for the last time,
"Casting all your care upon Him," and for
us to reply: "Yes! Yes! He careth for
us!" and then to fall asleep.

Sermons by Rev. J. Hullett.

...Once more, as to our proper place and proper state in this world. "The woman," that is, the Church, "fled into the wilderness." It is there, in the desert, that a place is prepared for her of God. It is there that her work lies, and it is there that her happiness will be found.

O, my brethren, it has been the misfortune, and it has been the misery, and it has been the sin, of the professed Church in all times, that she would not stay there! She would not rest where God had prepared a place for her! She would, in heart at least, turn back again into Egypt!

Or, if she could not get back, she would make her wilderness as like Egypt as possible; she would sit there, at one time depressed and languid, remembering the flesh-pots which were denied her; she would rise, at another time, and make her tents one vast bazaar, in which all the finery and all the luxury of Egypt should be simulated and parodied!

You all know how the Church has copied and flattered the world. You all know how unwilling our own individual hearts are to recognize and to acquiesce in our true position as strangers, pilgrims, sojourners, upon earth. It is no vain parable, which bids us remember who we are, and where—occupants of a shifting station, not dwellers in a permanent home. If, for us, "the Child," the Child Divine and human, the man Christ Jesus, has indeed been "caught up to God and to His Throne," then *there*, with Him, where He dwells, where He sitteth at God's right hand, there, and not here, is our home and our citizenship.

"If ye then be risen with Christ, seek those things which are above!"

Rev. Dr. Vaughan.

If sorrow came not near us, and the love
Which wisdom-working sorrow best imparts,
Found never time of entrance to our hearts,
If we had won already a safe shore,
Or if our changes were already o'er,
Our pilgrim being we might quite forget,
Our hearts but faintly on those mansions set,
Where there shall be no sorrow any more.
Therefore we will not be unwise to ask
This, nor secure exemption from our share
Of mortal sufferings, and life's drearier
    task—
Not this, but grace our portion so to bear,
That we may rest, when grief and pain are
    over,
"With the meek Son of our Almighty
    Lover."

DEAN TRENCH.

"Moab hath been at ease from his youth, and he hath settled on his lees, and hath not been emptied from vessel to vessel, neither hath he gone into captivity; therefore his taste remained in him, and his scent is not changed." Jer. xlviii. 11.

......The danger is, that, standing thus upon the lees from your youth, disturbed by no crosses, unsettled by no changes, you will finally become so fast rooted in pride and forgetfulness of God, as to miss everything most dear in existence. Nothing could be more perilous for you than just that which you deem your happiness. Nor is any word of God more pointedly serious than this,— "Because they have no changes, therefore they fear not God."

......Others, again, have been visited by many and great adversities, emptied about from vessel to vessel all their lives long, still wondering what it means, while still they adhere to their sins.

There is alas! no harder kind of life than this,—a life of continual discipline that really teaches nothing.

Is it so with you, or is it not? Scorched by all manner of adversities, are you still unpurified by the fires you have passed through?

Defeated, crossed, crushed, beaten out of every plan, baffled in every project, blasted in every object your soul has embraced, are you still unprofited? I have known such examples,—fig-trees that God has dug about every year, and that still remain as barren as if no hand of care had touched them.

Is there anything more strange, than that a man should be no wise instructed by the sufferings of a life,—separated in no degree from the world, and self, and the scent of his manifold evils, by that which God has sent upon him to correct his understanding, and purify his love, and fashion him even for the angelic glory? So he plods on still, contriving, and failing, and groping with his face downward, and wondering that the earth will not consent to bless him! Oh, poor, weather-worn, defeated, yet unprofited man,—he cannot see when good cometh! There is no class of beings more to be pitied than defeated men who have gotten nothing out of their defeat but that dry sorrow of the world which makes it only more barren, and therefore more insupportable......

......Do you find, my brother, that when you are thus emptied about, dislodged, agitated, loosened, you are purified; or, does the bad flavour of your worldly habits, the scent of your old ambition, or your earthly pride remain?

......A strange thing is it, that, having no great persecutions to suffer for Christ, you cannot find how, as a follower, to endure these common trials. God forbid that you so little understand your privilege in them...Bid them

welcome when they come; lift up your cry
unto God, and beseech Him that by any
means He will correct you, and purify you,
and separate you to Himself.

THE NEW LIFE.

He was houseless and homeless; He was
lonely in heart; He was falsely accused; He
was scorned and taunted and maligned; all
these things He received as His daily portion,
and saw in them the very cup of sorrow
which His Father gave for His drinking. But
when He saw another's soul sad or suffering or sorrow-laden, the sympathy which He
asked not for Himself was ever ready on His
part for another.

VAUGHAN'S "BOOK AND THE LIFE."

My soul, there is a countrie,
  Afar beyond the stars,
Where stands a wingèd sentrie,
  All skilful in the wars;
There, above noise and danger,
  Sweet peace sits crowned with smiles,
And one born in a manger
  Commands the beauteous files.
He is thy gracious Friend,
  And (Oh, my soul, awake!)
Did in pure love descend,
  To die here for thy sake.
If thou canst but get thither,
  There grows the flower of peace,
The rose that cannot wither,
  Thy fortress, and thy ease.
Leave then thy foolish ranges,
  For none can thee secure,
But One who never changes,
  Thy God, Thy Life, Thy Cure.

                              HENRY VAUGHAN.

One sweetly solemn thought
Comes to me o'er and o'er;
I'm nearer home to-day,
Than I've ever been before.

Nearer my Father's house
Where the many mansions be;
Nearer the great white throne,
Nearer the crystal sea.

Nearer the bound of life
Where we lay our burden down,
Nearer leaving the cross,
Nearer gaining the crown.

But lying daily between,
Winding down through the night
Is the deep and unknown stream,
That leads at last to the light.

Jesus, perfect my trust,
Strengthen the band of my faith;
Let me feel Thee near when I stand
On the edge of the shore of death.

Feel Thee near when my feet
Are slipping over the brink,
For it may be I'm nearer home,
Nearer now than I think.

Hymn.

A great sorrow recasts a soul; it either draws it nearer to the Friend whose intimacy must elevate it; or drives it into the far cold space of rebellion and despair. When the stripes of affliction are dealt to those whom God has called into His great school of work for souls, it is manifestly to give them new faculty in their calling. They needed to see deeper down into their own hearts, and thus into the hearts of others. Oh! how many a sorrow of the poor may we have striven to comfort, while their experiences have told them that we stood outside it! But the great leveller Death, has admitted us now into an inner circle of fellowship with the human family "born unto trouble."

True human loneliness is only found in living apart from God and His work. It has been said that "the infinite ocean of human woes makes every idle moment in a Christian's life guilt in the sight of God."

LIFE WORK.

N

Still onward as to Southern skies,
We spread our sail, new stars arise,
New lights upon the glancing tide,
Fresh hues where pearl and coral hide.

And we would daily, nightly draw
Nearer to Thee in love and awe,
Till in Love's home we pause at last,
Our anchor in the deep Heaven cast.

The while, across the changeful sea,
Feeling our way, we cling to Thee,
Unchanging Lord! and Thou dost mark
For each his Station in Thine Ark.

KEBLE.

I cannot praise Thee now, Lord,
  I cannot praise Thee now ;
For my heart is sorely riven,
  And a cloud is on my brow;
But Praise is waiting for Thee,
  In the glorious future Time,
Amid the bright revealings,
  When Zion's hill we climb.

I cannot praise Thee here, Lord,
  I cannot praise Thee here ;
For in my soul is sorrow,
  And in mine eye a tear;
But praise is waiting for Thee
  When the chequered past appears
In the sunshine of the future,
  All smiling through these tears.

I cannot praise Thee here, Lord,
   I cannot praise Thee here;
For my pathway lies through shadows,
   And my heart is lone and drear;
But Praise is waiting for Thee,
   When the pilgrimage is past,
And at our home in glory,
   We gather in at last.

And I will praise Thee here, Lord,
   When Zion's heights I gain;
But might I not be tuning
   A prelude to the strain?
While praise is waiting for Thee,
   Thou'lt lend a listening ear,
To its low and faint rehearsal,
   In faltering accents here!

Then let me praise Thee now, Lord,
  In the dark and cloudy day,
Though sad, and sore disquieted
  By reason of the way.
For the praise that's waiting for Thee
  Good cause shall yet appear,
And I'll wake the golden harp strings
  Beneath the falling tear.

ANON.

All God's providences, all God's dealings
with us, all His judgments, mercies, warnings,
deliverances, tend to peace and repose as
their ultimate issue. All our troubles and
pleasures here, all our anxieties, fears, doubts,
difficulties, hopes, encouragements, afflictions,
losses, attainments, tend this one way......
After the fever of life; after wearinesses, and
sicknesses ; fightings and despondings ; lan-
guor and fretfulness; struggling and failing,
struggling and succeeding, after all the
changes and chances of this troubled and
unhealthy state, at length comes death, at
length the White Throne of God, at length
the Beatific Vision.

NEWMAN'S SERMONS.

...And so, as you pass on, stage by stage, in your courses of experience, it is made clear to you that, whatever you have laid upon you to do or to suffer, whatever to want, whatever to surrender or to conquer, is exactly best for you.

* * * * * *

No room for a discouraged or depressed feeling, therefore, is left you. Enough that you exist for a purpose high enough to give meaning to life, and to support a genuine inspiration. If your sphere is outwardly humble, if it even appears to be quite insignificant, God understands it better than you do, and it is a part of His wisdom to bring out great sentiments in humble conditions, great principles in works that are outwardly trivial, great characters under great adversities and heavy loads of encumbrance. The tallest saints of God will often be those who walk in the deepest obscurity, and are even despised or quite overlooked by man. Let it be enough that God is in your history, and that the plan of your biography is His, the issue He has set for it, is the highest and the best. Away, then, O man, with thy feeble complaints, and feverish despondencies. If God is really preparing us all to become that which is the very highest and best thing possible, there ought never to be a discouraged or uncheerful being in the world.

THE NEW LIFE.

"Thou hast dealt well with Thy Servant."

Well, in seeking me, when I sought not
Thee.
Well, in giving what I have not asked.
Well, in refusing what I have asked.
Well, in calling me to the service of Thy
Church.
Well, in calling me to suffer instead of to
serve.
Well, in succouring me in temptation.
Well, in guiding my wandering feet.
Thou hast dealt mercifully with me when I
have sinned.
Bountifully with me when I have been
brought low.
Gently with me when I have been in trial.
Faithfully with me at all times.

REV. G. WAGNER.

...Nor speak I this of the death unto
sin, of which all my people must be par-
takers, as the inevitable result of their life
in me, but of the slaying, once for all,
sooner or later, in their career, of some
beloved hope, or love, or dream, which hath
been to them the dearest and most cherished,
and which ofttimes, for that same reason,
hath become a clog upon their heavenward
feet, and an obstacle between their souls
and me.

...When the blow is dealt, and the
memory of the dead joy is cold and mournful, as the thought of a corpse within its
tomb, then doth there pass into their souls
that which I labour to procure for them on
earth...even a desolation so utter and so
insupportable, that, with dim weeping eyes
and bursting heart, they stagger to my Cross,
and lay them down beneath it, with an
undivided longing henceforth to know no

other happiness, in time, or in eternity, save
my pure Love alone!

...Said I not even unto thee, that on
this earth thou mayest not linger, nor be
content, nor seek to lay thee down? Remember those words, "There remaineth
therefore a rest for the people of God."
Not here—not here, but in that Paradise
of pure delights, where I have gone to
prepare a place for those that love me.
Oh, my Child, take heed that no dream
beguile thee!...too soon shall it be to thee
as a drink of deadly wine, lulling thee to
slumber, when the very morn of thine eternal
day is breaking, and the goal about to burst
on thine enraptured eyes......Come unto me,
wounded and weeping, homeless and joyless,
outcast and alone,—come in tears, which
none will wipe away,—come in pain, which
no man will relieve,—come in agony, which
all shall pass unheeding, and I—I will give
thee rest.

DIVINE MASTER.

...And a martyr thou shalt be, but in
my own chosen way, even in all the common
duties of thy sphere, never neglected through
weariness and gloom, but never winning
human praise, as deeds of high devotion
would.

...Who gave thee that Cross, which I now
find thee seeking to diminish, with such
self-willed ardour? Was I then ignorant
of its nature, when I laid it on thee? Had
I no knowledge of its sharpness?......Stretch
forth thy hands, and I will guide thee;
stretch them forth in prayer for light and
truth, and both will ever come to thee.
Light, to shine upon each step which thou
must take from day to day; and Truth, to
pierce into the depths of thy weak soul...

"Me ye have not," I said, "but the poor
ye have with you always," and faithfully
have I performed that promise; there is not
a spot in the wide world, unblest by some

poor struggling sufferer, who claims from my redeemed the care and tenderness they would bestow on me. There is thy work, my Child, enough to occupy each moment of thy life.

If nought else is left thee, thou canst go forth and give them Love! that which above all other things I claim from thee. Go to them in their sickness and affliction—weep with them that weep—rejoice with them that rejoice;—thine be the voice of comfort in the hour of trial—of tenderness in the time of desolation,...and to all, for my dear sake—a servant.

THE DIVINE MASTER.

Not only, the dead are the living, but
since they have died, they live a better life
than ours...In what particulars is their life
now higher than it was? First, they have
close fellowship with Christ; then, they are
separated from this present body of weakness,
of dishonour, of corruption; then, they are
withdrawn from all the trouble, and toil, and
care of this present life; and then, and surely
not least, they have got death behind them,
not having that awful figure standing on their
horizon waiting for them to come up with it
...They are closer to Christ; they are delivered from the body, as a source of weakness;
as a hinderer of knowledge; as a dragger-
down of all the aspiring tendencies of the
soul; as a source of sin; as a source of pain;
they are delivered from all the necessity of
labour which is agony, of labour which is
disproportionate to strength, of labour which

often ends in disappointment, of labour which is wasted so often in mere keeping life in, of labour which at the best is a curse, though it be a merciful curse too; they are delivered from that 'fear of death' which, though it be stripped of its sting, is never extinguished in any soul of man that lives; and they can smile at the way in which that narrow and inevitable passage bulked so large before them all their days, and, after all, when they come to it was so slight and small. If these be parts of the life of them that 'sleep in Jesus'; if they are fuller of knowledge, fuller of wisdom, fuller of love, and capacity of love, and object of love; fuller of holiness, fuller of energy and yet full of rest from head to foot; if all the hot tumult of earthly experience is stilled and quieted, all the fever beating of this blood of ours ever at an end; all the 'whips and arrows of outrageous fortune' done with for ever, and if the calm face which we looked upon, and out of which the lines of

✠

sorrow and pain, and sickness melted away, giving it back a nobler nobleness than we had ever seen upon it in life is only an image of the restful and more blessed being into which they have passed,—if the dead are thus, then 'Blessed are the dead'.

Rev. A. McLaren.

For a long time I felt myself to be a lost sheep, not knowing on whom to rely; and now with the deepest consciousness that I have at last attained rest, I exclaim, "The Lord is my Shepherd!" What is there that can harm me? I have reached the harbour, and storms can no more drive my little vessel afloat upon the wide sea. And as I look forward into the future, I exclaim with David, "I shall not want."

THORLUCK'S HOME OF DEVOTION.

o

...My brethren, every one of us has the offer, of being thus led, thus watched over, thus provided for, thus reclaimed. For every one of us the Good Shepherd has already given His own life. Words cannot describe the minuteness of that care with which we believe every life to be overlooked and guarded by Him who has all power in Heaven and in Earth. When a Christian towards the close of life looks back upon his pilgrimage as a whole and in its parts, the only way in which he can describe it is that suggested by the words of scripture, "*God hath led me* all these years." I see it now so plainly; how there has been a hand over me, the hand of a real and living Person, giving this, and withholding that, both alike for good; placing me, perhaps where I would not, and then showing me that it had been well; not suffering me to forget, or else recalling me to recollection; denying me, or else taking away from me, something on which my heart was too much set, and then giving me something else which, because less desired, was safer; chastening me when I fell away, and often by sharp and painful strokes bringing me back to Himself. Doubtless Heaven will be full of such remembrances of earthly life, each remembrance ending in the ascription of praise. And cannot earth anticipate these recollections, these ascriptions of praise? Yes, the youngest life has had some such experiences; middle life has them in abundance; Oh how we forget God when we are in prosperity! when life smiles on us, how do we think scorn, as it were, of the pleasant land beyond; how do we provoke God by our murmurings; how do we dishonour Him by setting our affection on things below. ...When He slays us, we seek Him, as it is written; when He hides His face, we humble ourselves; when He delivers us again, we sing His praise: but within a

while we forget His works; we live care-
lessly; we scarcely pray; we cleave to the
dust of this world; again the stroke falls;
again we repent; again we amend; alas,
again it is a shortlived effort;—and in many
such backslidings, and a few such returns,
life slips away; the call comes, and is the
door still open?

My brethren, God is leading you, offering
at least to lead you, all your life long; and
O the safety, O the happiness, O the deep
peace, of those who early accept that offer!
...Every morning let your prayer be, *Lord,
lead me*....If I stray, follow me into the
desert and recal me. If I faint, carry me in
Thy bosom. When I walk at last through
the valley of the shadow of death, be Thou
with me. Let Thy goodness and mercy
follow me all the days of my life, and then
let me dwell in Thy house for ever.

Dr Vaughan's Memorials of Harrow Sundays.

Is then Despair the end of all our woe?
Far off the angel voices answer, No!
Devils despair, for they believe and tremble;
But man believes and hopes. Our griefs
    resemble
Each other but in this. Grief comes from
    heaven;
Each thinks his own the bitterest trial given;
Each wonders at the sorrows of his lot;
His neighbour's sufferings presently forgot,
Though wide the difference which our eyes
    can see
Not only in grief's kind, but its degree.
God grants to some, all joys for their
    possession;
Nor loss, nor cross the favoured mortal
    mourns;
While some toil on, outside those bounds
    of blessing,
Whose weary feet for ever tread on thorns.

But over all our tears God's rainbow bends;
To all our cries a pitying ear He lends;
Yea, to the feeble sound of man's lament,
How often have His messengers been sent!
No barren glory circles round His throne.
By mercies' errands were His angels known:
Where hearts were heavy, and where eyes
    were dim,
There did the brightness radiate from Him;
God's pity—clothed in an apparent form,
Starred with a polar light the human storm,
Floated o'er tossing seas man's sinking bark,
And for all dangers built one sheltering ark.

MRS NORTON.

Ah! when the infinite wisdom of life de-
scendeth upon us,
Crushes to earth our hope, and under the
earth, in the grave-yard;
Then it is good to pray unto God: for His
sorrowing children
Turns He ne'er from His door, but He
heals, and helps, and consoles them.

LONGFELLOW.

Man of woman is born in travail, to live in misery: man through Christ doth die in joy, and live in felicity. He is born to die, and dieth to live. Strait as he cometh into the world, with cries he uttereth his miserable estate; strait as he departeth, with songs he praiseth God for ever. Scarce yet in his cradle, three deadly enemies assault him: after death no adversary may annoy him. Whilst he is here, he displeaseth God; when he is dead, he fulfilleth His will. In this life here he dieth through sin; in the life to come he liveth in His righteousness. Through many tribulations in earth he is still purged; with joy unspeakable in heaven is he made pure for ever. Here he dieth every hour; there he liveth continually. Here is sin; there is righteousness. Here is time; there is eternity.

Here is hatred; there is love. Here is pain; there is pleasure. Here is misery; there is felicity. Here is corruption; there is immortality. Here we see vanity; there shall we behold the majesty of God with triumphant and unspeakable joy in life everlasting.

THE MARTYR BARTLETT GREEN, 1556.

When your Heavenly Father sets a crown
of thorns upon the heads of all His sons, of
all those whom He designs heirs of immortality, what would you think, if He should
pass by your heads?   Might it not make you
doubt, that you were no sons, but bastards?

You lose nothing, while you are suffering;
for this is not the season for any other thing.

Nay, if you have not troubles in the flesh,
you lose your season.   Would you have it so,
that for a little vain ease, or pleasure in this
world, you, among all the saints, when you
come into Heaven, should say, "I have lost
one season, which can never be recovered.
There is *one* state of divine appearances, *one*
discovery of God, which I am unacquainted
with, and can never behold, because I have
slipt the season for it"?

                                        STERRY.

When Hannah had prayed, she had peace; she was no more troubled. I cannot say that God let her know that *her* will should be *His*. But this I know, that *His* will was now made *hers*. This resignation was her rest. The soul tost with a tempest prays, and puts into the will of God, as to a harbour. Here she lies sheltered from every storm. The will of God is a perpetual calm: for there are no cross-tides, nor contrary winds. The spirit that rides by prayer in the haven of God's will, is fenced from violent blasts, by the power and wisdom of God, as high and mighty rocks on each side.

STERRY.

Now while they were thus drawing towards the gate, behold a company of the heavenly host came out to meet them; to whom it was said by the other two shining ones, "These are the men that have loved our Lord, when they were in the world, and that have left all for His Holy Name; and He hath sent us to fetch them, and we have brought them thus far on their desired journey, that they may go in and look their Redeemer in the face with joy."...

...And now were these two men, as it were, in Heaven, before they came at it, being swallowed up with a sight of angels and with hearing of their melodious notes... But, above all, the warm and joyful thoughts that they had about their own dwelling there with such company, and that for ever and ever, Oh, by what tongue or pen can their glorious joy be expressed?...

Now, just as the gates were opened to let in the men, I looked in after them; and behold the City shone like the sun, the

streets also were paved with gold, and in
them walked many men with crowns on
their heads, palms in their hands, and golden
harps, to sing praises withal:...And after
that they shut up the gates: which when
I had seen, I wished myself amongst them.

PILGRIM'S PROGRESS.

There he waits for his release,
There in God finds perfect peace;
Till the long years end at last,
And he too at length has past
From the sorrow and the fears,
From the anguish and the tears,
From the desolate distress
Of this world's great loneliness,
From its withering and its blight,
From the shadow of its night,
Into God's pure sunshine bright.

DEAN TRENCH.

Child. But Oh! what means this weakness, and this dim bewilderment? For I feel as though some mighty change were working in me. The former things are passed away, and behold, all things are becoming new! I see no more the world, and the glories of it, as they appear unto the eye of mortal man, but in a light so clear and awful! Surely it beameth from eternity itself! How vain and perishing hath that world become, thus suddenly unveiled to me!

Divine Master. Rise up, my Child, my faithful one, and come away; for lo, the winter is past, the rain is over and gone, the shadows depart of thy mortal life, and the day is dawning that never shall fade. It is past—it is gone—the dark time of thy conflict and trial...the time of the singing of Angels is come for thee, and the voice of the Seraphim is heard in that land. Thou hast wrestled with sin, till the breaking of the day; thou hast toiled all night, but the morning is nigh. Arise up then, my Child, my faithful one, and come away, let us haste and be gone, for the dawn is bright on the everlasting hills.

Child. Oh, my Lord, in the time past of my life, there was a great strong wind that rent my soul, and brake in pieces all my hopes in this world...but Thou wert not in the wind...and after the wind there was an earthquake...all the fair things of earth I had sought to repose in, gave way beneath my feet, and I knew of what dust they were made;...but Thou wert not in the earthquake...Then there was a fire, the searching flame of suffering, fierce and intense...but Thou wert not in the fire...and I still lived on; and now there is a still small voice...

Divine Master. And I am here! Thy Master is come, and calleth for thee...... My Child, the day breaketh, and we must depart; the shadow of death is darkening on thine eyelids, and the radiance of earthly suns hath passed from them for ever......But the Hand that once opened the eyes of the blind, is laid upon thine: and through thy soul, already trembling on the threshold of a new existence, the light of Eternity is dawning, ere yet the silver cord that binds thy mortal life is altogether loosed. Look up—what seest thou?

Child. I see worlds floating in the infinite glory of God, like motes in the sunshine; I see the centuries falling into the ocean of Eternity, swift as the rain-drops in summer.

Divine Master. Look again—what seest thou?

Child. The word—the word is fulfilled. Mine eyes behold the King in His beauty. Oh God, THOU ART LOVE!

THE DIVINE MASTER.

THE END.

CAMBRIDGE: PRINTED AT THE UNIVERSITY PRESS.

www.ingramcontent.com/pod-product-compliance
Lightning Source LLC
Chambersburg PA
CBHW030133030726
47498CB00007B/2690